FORBIDDEN MIDLIFE MATE

MARKED OVER FORTY

MEG RIPLEY

SHIFTER NATION

CONTENTS

FORBIDDEN MIDLIFE MATE

FORBIDDEN MIDLIFE MATE

MARKED OVER FORTY

1

"Happy freaking New Year to me," Lori Jensen muttered, poking at the touchscreen of her new fitness tracker. She'd just gotten it, and even though everyone made them sound so easy to use, she hadn't quite figured the thing out yet. At forty-eight, she was experiencing the joys of perimenopause, and her doctor had pushed her to start moving more to ease her symptoms. Exercise wouldn't stop her hot flashes, but she'd hoped it would at least get her energy and mood back on track. She couldn't use the excuse of being a busy mom anymore now that Conner was in college.

"Oh, hell. Jogging is still good for me even if the damn thing doesn't keep track of it." Slamming her car door and making sure she had her keys tucked in her pocket, Lori got started.

Eugene was new to her, and not a city she'd picked for herself. It was... *different*, that was for sure. Everyone seemed to be outside all the time, and she couldn't blame them, with the mild winter weather and all. It felt odd to be outdoors in January without a heavy parka, a hat, and thick gloves, but she had to remind herself she wasn't in Chinook, Montana anymore.

She wasn't the only one out for a jog that day. The wide gravel paths were bustling with people. Parents walked with their small children, who dragged them off to a nearby playground. A bicyclist or two rode by, and Lori picked up her pace. She was tired, but that wasn't going to stop her. She could do this.

"Excuse us!"

Lori bolted to the right as a group of fit young college girls came darting past. While Lori had donned her sweats and a dingy old bra, these girls were slim and lithe in their stylish athletic wear, showing off their perfect shapes in their clingy leggings, form-fitting sports bras, and cropped hoodies. Their ponytails wagged as they passed by, mocking Lori for going so slow.

She snorted to herself, remembering how she, too, had once been young and lithe, thinking she'd remain that way forever. "Enjoy it while it lasts, ladies. Gravity's a bitch."

A loud beep had her looking down at her fitness tracker. It was finally working, or at least she was pretty sure it was. She had no clue what all the numbers and symbols meant, but it was obviously doing something. Good. She was really doing this. Not just the jog, but everything. This was the start of a whole new life for Lori, and she was determined to make the most of it.

Her muscles burned, reminding her that all the years of running the saloon with Chuck hadn't been the same as getting proper exercise every day, even though she'd spent most of her shifts entirely on her feet. Of course, she probably wouldn't have had to bust her ass so much if Chuck had bothered to do his job.

It was supposed to be fifty-fifty when they'd first opened The Wagon Wheel. It had always been Chuck's dream, but he'd never had the money. Lori had just been given a small inheritance from a great-uncle, but the fact that the man she'd loved wanted her to be involved in his business had been sweet and flattering. They'd bought the cheapest old building in Chinook and transformed it from a sad little wreck on the outskirts of town to a hopping saloon everyone clambered to on the weekends. Even the weekdays weren't too dull once Lori had talked Chuck into doing theme nights and serving better food. People were bored in their little town, so they loved the chance to see their friends over a beer while playing darts. They loved it even more when there were holiday parties, charity events, and pool tournaments.

But as hard as she'd worked, nothing was quite good enough for Chuck. Lori thought she'd made him happy, but she knew she was wrong when he ran off with the hostess.

Lori had let her mind completely wander, and with a jolt, she realized she'd gone way further than she'd ever thought she would. She glanced at the tracker on her wrist, wondering if she really had gone over a mile. That would explain why her lungs burned. Lori slowed to a brisk walk. She could feel her heart thumping, but it wasn't setting her device off, so it couldn't have been too bad.

Lori grinned. This really was a whole new start for her. This wasn't the kind of thing she would've done if she'd stayed back in Chinook, listening to all the locals whisper behind their hands about how

Chuck had run off, thinking she didn't hear them. She'd never been happier about moving away because the last thing she wanted was for anyone to think she was doing this just to get back at Chuck. It didn't have a damn thing to do with him, nor did anything else in her life. She was finally *free.*

A black shape fluttered in front of her. Lori turned to follow it, spotting the raven just as it landed in the grass on the other side of the path. It cocked its head to the side, studying her.

"Well, hello." She paused, knowing she couldn't stay still for too long and lose her momentum, but it had so much personality. "You look like you're trying to tell me something."

It opened its thick black beak and let out a jittering call before moving a few steps away from her.

"Oh, it's okay. I'm not trying to hurt you. I've always liked animals. I mean, it's not like I have any pets right now. I just moved here, and my landlord doesn't allow them."

Another cry issued from the raven's throat just before it flew into the air, swooped between a few trees, and settled into a low branch.

"I wish I knew what you were saying." But something inside her knew the bird wanted her to follow it. Lori had always felt animals knew far more than people, and she'd been looking for signs to let her know she was heading in the right direction by moving out to Eugene. Perhaps the raven was telling her just that.

When she reached the base of the tree, the raven swept off for another one.

The trail was getting narrower. Lori realized she hadn't seen any joggers or cyclists for a while, and the trees were thicker there. Fear began to bloom in her chest, thinking perhaps she'd wandered too far, but she dismissed it. What's the worst thing that could happen by getting in touch with nature a little?

"Caw!" the raven insisted.

"All right, all right! What's so important?" Lori laughed. She left the trail behind as she followed the raven up the hill, wondering what Conner would say when she told him the story. He'd probably shake his head and ask her not to repeat it in front of his football buddies. The raven led her all the way up the hill, insistent as ever until they reached the top.

Then it was silent.

"You finally ran out of things to say?" she asked.

But the bird wasn't looking at her anymore. It

peered down the other side of the hill, its head twitching a little to one side.

Lori looked, wondering if the raven had spotted its next snack. When she turned, she realized the two of them weren't alone. A group of people had gathered near the base of the hill on the other side. There had to be at least twenty of them. They sat around and spoke in hushed tones so Lori didn't hear anything they were saying. Given where she was in the country, Lori figured it was a hippie gathering or something. She wasn't going to bother them, but something caught her eye just as she started to turn away.

Looking back, Lori realized a dog was moving toward the group. No, not a dog. A *wolf*. It trotted up from the thicker part of the woods beyond the hill, its eyes yellow and determined. Her heart lurched in her chest. It was beautiful, the kind of thing she'd love to see up close, but it was coming right at them. Lori sucked in a breath to yell at the group, to tell them to get out of there.

But one of the men turned toward the wolf, then became one himself.

Lori blinked. That wasn't right. She hadn't just seen that. She glanced down at her fitness tracker, wondering if she'd overdone it and was now hallucinating. Leaning against the nearest tree for balance, Lori looked back down the hill. The man who'd been there a moment ago was gone, just as she thought, and now there were two wolves. They weren't sneaking up on the people, though. They were right there in the midst of them.

It couldn't be right, but the rest began to transform. Their faces stretched into long muzzles as their heads writhed on their shoulders. They fell forward onto all fours as thick gray fur sprouted on their bodies. Her gut twisted, but she couldn't look away. She caught glimpses of them between various forms of human and beast.

A scream ripped through the air. When the wolves all looked in her direction, she knew it was coming from her.

Lori froze, watching in horror as the pack of wolves raced up the hill. Their claws dug into the soft earth as they bounded for her, a stream of fur that moved and ran around each other without the least bit of trouble. They were gaining on her, and quickly.

"Holy shit!" Sucking in a breath, Lori scrambled back down the hill. It was steeper than she remembered it being on the way up. Her shins screamed at her to slow down. She wasn't used to all this exercise. But her brain sent an extra flood of adrenaline through her system, and she would deal with the aches and pains later.

Lori flung herself down the hill, then hit flatter land and barreled back toward the trail. She only had to get there, then someone would come along. Someone would've heard her screams and was probably on their way. Right?

She could hear the wolves, their panting breaths becoming louder by the second. She knew they had to be gaining on her, and her spine tingled in terrible anticipation. But she had to keep going. She wasn't going to give up.

Her toe caught on a root, and she pitched forward. The raven called once more as the world went black.

———

Lori slowly opened her eyes. She felt as though she'd been swimming in a deep black void for hours, and it hurt to let even the slightest bit of light in. Squinting against the painful light, Lori tried to turn her head to the side, but it hurt too much.

"Hey, there. Are you with us?" a deep voice

asked. It was rough but kind, and it sounded like it was coming from the other end of a tunnel.

She moved her mouth, trying to answer, but she didn't know how. Her mind groped around for thoughts and found none. "What... what happened?" she croaked.

"You hit your head, but you're all right now. Just take it easy." It was that same voice again, but this time it was closer.

She opened her eyes and looked up to see a rugged, handsome face. Piercing blue eyes stared down into hers, his brows wrinkled in concern. She didn't recognize him, but something within her told her she knew him.

"There you are," he said gently as she started to come to a little more. "You'll be fine."

Lori wasn't entirely sure she agreed with him.

2

"AND SHE'S OUT AGAIN." REX STUDIED THE WOMAN ON his couch.

"That's just as well," Dawn remarked. She fished around in a bag she'd brought in with her. "That'll give me time to get the tincture made. Don't try to bring her out of it again."

"I wasn't trying to in the first place." Rex's eyes flashed silver as he returned his gaze to the stranger. When the clan had brought her in, Rex had been fully immersed in sampling a few local bands for Selene's. He loved that he could just open his laptop, put on a pair of headphones, and audition dozens of bands without them knowing it. The only problem was that he tended to get lost in the process, and he hadn't realized how long he'd been at it.

"I don't know why you're trying to do anything with her at all." Dave had been pacing the room like a caged animal ever since the woman's arrival. "They shouldn't have brought her here. She's obviously human."

"Yes." Rex had to agree with that. He could smell it all over her, but something about it piqued his wolf's interest. "I don't think that means she's dangerous."

"They're all dangerous if you ask me."

"No one *did* ask you." Dawn shot Dave a look as she set several vials on a nearby table.

Rex let one side of his mouth creep up. His sister had always been one to speak her mind, regardless of the other person's pack status.

"Just take her out and be done with it," Dave snapped. He continued to pace, his fists curled at his sides, his jaw clenched. "She's going to wake up, figure out what's going on, and then have us all in a fucking government lab somewhere."

Dawn let out a derisive snort. "You're just paranoid. Maybe you should start taking something for that."

Dave narrowed his eyes.

"Human or not, there's no need to take an innocent life if there's another option," Rex said. "Dawn is making one of her tinctures, so this woman won't remember a thing." He, however, would remember every detail. He hadn't been able to take his eyes off her since she'd arrived. The way her delicate eyebrows arched, the way her full lips trembled slightly as her mind fought to return to consciousness. Something about her was utterly captivating.

"Innocent?" Dave demanded. "She was spying on us."

"Hardly," Dawn scoffed. "Look at her. Do you not see the sweatsuit and fitness tracker? She was jogging through the park. She probably got lost and just stumbled across you guys. That's what you get for shifting at the far edge of the property like a bunch of idiots."

"How dare you speak to me that way!" Dave charged toward her, nearly making her knock her vials off the table. "You're lucky you're the Alpha's sister!"

"And the Alpha is right here," Rex reminded him, stepping away from the human long enough to get between his third in command and his sister. He drew himself to his full height and let his broad shoulders spread wide. "Dawn is right. It was probably just an accident, and we're only going to bring more attention to ourselves. This is the safer way to do things. More importantly, it's the way that *I* want to do things."

"Fine, but let it be known that I think this is a shitty idea. You're going to bring something terrible down on our pack by letting her go." Without another word, Dave stormed out of the room.

Rex let him go and returned his attention to the woman. "Do you think you'll be able to erase her memory completely?"

Swirling a small glass vial between her fingers, Dawn cast him a curious look. "Did you let him get to you?"

"No. I've just had my own doubts, but I wouldn't tell Dave that. He's too eager to do something drastic." As he looked down at their guest, he knew he couldn't possibly follow through on Dave's advice, even if Dawn's magic didn't work. Rex studied her again as Dawn came around behind her head. His wolf tugged at him, but he didn't understand why.

Pulling a chair up next to the couch so she could be comfortable, Dawn looked at the human and sighed. "Selene's blood, Rex. I know why you called me in here. I mean, I've got healing magic from Mom's side and work as a nurse all day. But now that Dave is gone, I have to admit I'm a little squeamish about having a human in the packhouse. You know people are going to talk."

"Since when have I given a damn about what anyone says?" Rex knew his right to the position of Alpha was one that he solidly deserved. His parents had ruled this pack for a long time, and his grandparents had before them. No one could question his authority.

She shrugged. "Fair enough. I'm certainly not voting for harming her, but I'm just saying some might not be thrilled about your little catch-and-release program."

"It'll be fine. Of course, the sooner we get this done, the sooner she'll be on her way home." He rolled his hand through the air to encourage her to start.

Dawn nodded. She closed her eyes and took a deep breath, the fine lines around her eyes relaxing a bit as she dropped her shoulders. Rex didn't know how her gifts worked, only that they did. The healing magic that ran through the women in their family was strong, and they knew how to wield it. Slowly and deliberately, she rubbed the oil-based tincture on the woman's forehead. The words she muttered were incomprehensible to him, but Rex knew he didn't need to hear or understand them for the spell to work. He felt the electric energy of her magic in the air, and a moment later, she was done.

"So, can I wake her up now?" he asked impatiently.

Dawn gave him another curious look, but she shrugged. "That's entirely up to you. Get her talking, and you'll probably bring her back pretty quickly. I'm going to wash my hands and see if Dave stirred up trouble elsewhere in the packhouse. Let me know if you need anything else." She took her bag and slipped out of the room.

Rex hesitated as he stood over the woman. She wasn't an intruder, considering she'd been brought in unconscious. He agreed with Dawn's assertion that this woman's sighting had been an accident. It was the only thing that made sense. Still, her presence felt heavy to him. Rex couldn't explain why, but his wolf was restless as hell. It was trying to tell him something about her, but there was nothing to tell. She was just a human.

"Hey." He shook her shoulder gently, hoping he was doing the right thing. "Hey, it's time to wake up."

She moaned a little, sending a shiver down his spine.

He clenched his teeth and told himself he was just feeling off because a human was in there among his packmates. It was a dangerous situation, but probably not in the way Dave thought it was. "Wake up. You need to come back."

Her eyes fluttered. They opened just a crack, revealing only a slit of her brown eyes. They were a few shades darker than the butterscotch waves of her hair. Her breathing quickened, and she winced in pain. "My head."

"You're all right, though." He remembered what Dawn had said about keeping her talking. How was he supposed to make conversation with this stranger? "You hit your head while you were jogging in the park."

Her eyes squeezed shut, making him worry that she was slipping off again, but then she opened them more fully. Her gaze instantly focused on him, and Rex could see the minute movements of her facial muscles as thoughts and emotions flickered across her mind. "What?"

"You tripped and hit your head while you were in the park," he repeated, knowing that having an alternate story to the one Dawn had erased would only help. "My friends brought you inside. My sister's a nurse, and she's already had a look at you. She said you're going to be fine."

"Oh." Uncertainty continued to dance over her face. "And who are you?"

Her eyes focused entirely on him. Rex felt as though she were holding him in place. It was the sort of thing his wolf would normally fight adamantly against, but not this time. It was already pulling toward her, being even more insistent than before. He swiped a hand over his face. "My name is Rex. I don't live far from the park. What's your name?" It was all simple enough and didn't really give anything away.

"Lori." A bit of that confusion lifted, and she swallowed. "Lori Jensen."

"Let me get you some water." He quickly moved to the small fridge on the other side of the room and grabbed a bottle of water, cracking it open for her. "You'll want to sit up, but you'd better do that slowly."

He put a hand on her shoulder to help her as she propped herself up on the couch, and that sizzle of energy that went up his arm was hard to ignore. Rex did, though. There had never been a human in the packhouse before. That was all it was.

"Thank you." She sipped the water with shaking hands. "I'm so sorry."

"Sorry? About what?"

"I don't know. I guess for hitting my head." She laughed, but she stopped and pressed her palm to her temple. "And now I'm sorry I laughed. I've got one hell of a headache."

He wanted to laugh, but he bit his tongue to keep it at bay. What would everyone think if they heard the two of them laughing it up in there? He didn't give a shit what they thought, but that didn't mean he was going to create chaos in his pack for no reason. "What do you remember?" Maybe it wasn't fair to test her so quickly after she'd woken up, and he certainly trusted that Dawn knew what she was doing. Still, he'd feel much better if he knew her status before he let her go.

"Um." She blinked again and took another sip of water. Then came a deep breath that made her buxom chest rise and fall. Rex tried not to look. "I drove to the park and went for a jog. God, it feels like that was days ago. Then there was this bird."

"A bird?" At least it wasn't a wolf. And why did she have to look so enticing? She was just wearing sweatpants and a sweatshirt, but they draped around her curves in a way that made him want to reach toward her and—

"Yeah. A raven. I followed it off the path, which was probably a dumb idea. I must have been watching it instead of where I was going." She took another sip of water. "I'm sorry. Where did you say I am again?"

"At my house. I don't live far from the park." He was repeating himself, but he had doubts about how much she had retained.

"Okay." She looked around and patted down her body, finally producing her cell phone from the pocket of her sweats. "I don't know if I'm up for driving at the moment, so I'll just call my son and see if he can pick me up if you'll give me your address."

"No, that's all right. I'll take you home." Rex could see that she was having trouble looking at her phone screen anyway, which gave him the perfect excuse to take her wrist and gently lay her hand on the couch cushion. There was that zing of energy again, but it was only because she made him uneasy. He needed to get her out of there.

"I don't want to be a burden."

"You're not. Not at all," he insisted. "It's the least I can do. Where do you live?"

Lori's face went completely blank.

Rex waited a few seconds, but when she still didn't say anything, he started to worry. Just how much had Dawn erased? If she'd somehow gone too far, this would be a difficult incident to recover from. "Do you remember your address?" he coached.

"I'm sorry. I'm trying. You see, I just moved to this new apartment. Hell, I just moved to this state." She let out an embarrassed little laugh. "It's like my brain is looking for it, but it's just not there."

"Do you have your driver's license with you?" Rex knew he had to get her out of the packhouse. For her sake. For the pack's. For his own. He didn't know what was happening to him. If this had been another wolf, he might have thought this was the fated pull shifters always talk about. But his mother had told him countless times about the vision she saw for him, and she'd always gone on and on about how his mate would be someone very special. At forty-five, he had yet to meet this special person, but Joan Glenwood wouldn't be saying that about a human.

"No. I don't have my wallet with me. It's in the car." Panic made her breathing speed up.

"Maybe a drive would help," he suggested, reaching out his hand to help her up. She could call someone and ask them, but that would just bring more questions and more attention to the pack. "You might see something familiar."

"Okay." She followed him through the house and

out into the garage, where he held open the passenger side door of his truck.

The overhead lights in the garage illuminated a row of vintage cars, and Lori pointed to them. "You're into classic cars, I take it?"

He had no need for inane conversation. He only needed to get her back where she belonged. Then he could return to the packhouse, remind Dave of his place, and move on with his life as though this had never happened. "No. They're my dad's."

"Oh. You live with your parents?"

"It's more like they live with me." Rex tried not to growl the answer. Shit. Why did he have to explain anything to this human? But he knew he needed to play nice if he wanted to get out of this situation unscathed.

"I'm not judging or anything," Lori said as they backed out of the garage and she got a look at the house. "I mean, housing here in Eugene is expensive. Just renting something has been ridiculous, and if I could live with family and split the cost, I would. I didn't think I would ever find something I could afford. Wait!"

He slammed on the brakes as he pulled out onto the road. Rex's heart hammered. "What?"

"I remember! It's on West Broadway." She

grinned as though she'd just won the lottery.

In a way, maybe she had. He could get her home, and no one else in the pack would know exactly where that was. "Good. I'll start heading that way."

They drove for a few minutes before she spoke again. "I really am sorry about all of this. I appreciate everything you've done."

"No problem." He made his way through mild traffic, ready for it all to be over with, but it was hard to concentrate on the road with her there beside him. Rex could easily reach out and lay a hand on her thigh. Why the hell did he want to do that? "I hear a bit of an accent. Where did you move from?"

She laughed, and though she touched her head once again at least it didn't stop her from laughing this time. "Chinook, Montana."

"Can't say I've ever heard of that town."

"You wouldn't. It's just a flash of buildings as you're driving through on the highway. Everything is very different here."

"How is that?" Rex tightened his grip on the wheel and slowed down, making sure he took the right turn. This woman was distracting.

"Well, for one thing, if I fell and hit my head out in Chinook, someone would probably still come and scrape me up like you did. The difference is that everyone in town would know about it before I came to, and they'd all have a different theory about why it happened. People here seem to mind their own business a little more."

She had no idea just how amusing that statement was, considering how many shifters were in these parts, just trying to keep an old family secret. "The gossip mill is churning there, I take it?"

"Definitely," Lori agreed. "It was one of the reasons I left."

He didn't care, and he shouldn't. He just needed to keep her talking so he knew she was okay. That way, when he dropped her off at her place, he'd never have any reason to wonder if he'd done the right thing. "Did people have a reason to gossip about you?"

"Well, I..." She trailed off and pressed her lips together. "People will always find something to talk about when they're bored enough. The biggest reason I moved here is for my son. He got a football scholarship from Eugene University. Oh. I should've just called him. He could've picked me up and saved you the trouble of not only driving me but waiting for me to figure out where the hell I live."

"It's no trouble at all," he reiterated. "This is it, right?"

Relief relaxed her shoulders as she looked at the apartment building he'd just pulled up in front of. She turned to him fully before she got out. "I owe you for this."

"No, you don't."

"Well, I still think I do, even if you don't." Those gorgeous brown eyes danced over his face for a moment as she smiled. "It was very nice to meet you, Rex."

He held out his hand without thinking, and this time, he anticipated the tremor that started at his palm when she touched it and bolted straight up his arm.

"Thank you again." She climbed out and headed up the walkway.

Rex watched her for a moment, telling himself he was only making sure she got into the building safely. That's what anyone would do, especially for someone that'd just been injured in the most remote part of the park and couldn't even remember her address. As soon as she was inside, he threw the truck in reverse. He shoved the gas pedal down as he got back onto the road.

His wolf was going rabid inside him. It'd been trying to tell him something, but he didn't know what.

3

"ARE YOU SHITTING ME?"

Lori sat on her couch and gazed out the window. It didn't look like January at all, or at least not the sort of January she was used to. The morning was cool and misty, but there was still some color and vibrance to the world. Days like this in Montana would be either the color of snow or mud with little in between. "I'm not. I wish I were, but I'm definitely not."

Abbie laughed. "You just keep having the best luck, don't you?"

Grabbing her laptop off the coffee table, Lori shook her head. "That's a nice way of putting it. At least the guy was hot, so there's that."

"Oh, tell me!"

"I don't know." It'd been so long since she'd felt she could just come right out and say a guy was good-looking. She'd been with Chuck for years. While it wasn't as though she didn't notice a handsome stranger here or there, it'd been more like admiring a piece of artwork. This Rex guy was a little different. "He was big, for one thing. He's probably the kind that goes to the gym every day and eats a dozen eggs for breakfast. And he had these killer blue eyes that just stared straight into my soul."

"So, is there something going on between the two of you?" Abbie teased. "Did you get his number or anything?"

Lori laughed and shook her head, although the echo of her headache still lurked in her skull, and she regretted doing it. She'd been friends with Abbie ever since junior high, and now it felt like they were right back in school again. "No, I didn't get his number. I don't even know his last name."

"You know where he lives, though," she teased.

"I was still pretty zonked when he drove me home, so I don't know about that. Oh, and then when I did get home, I had to call Conner and ask him to help me get my car since I'd left it at the park. I think he was a little freaked out about the whole thing."

"You probably could've just called an Uber or something," Abbie noted.

"Oh." That would've kept her from having to explain her predicament to her son, embarrassing as it was. "I didn't even think of that."

"Well, it isn't like we have it here in Chinook," Abbie noted. "But it's all right. I mean, you did move there to be with Conner. He's your backup."

"That's true." It'd been one hell of a decision to leave everything she'd ever known behind, but she reminded herself constantly that it was worth it. She wanted to keep a close relationship with him even if he was a college student trying to find himself.

"How's the job hunt going?"

"Meh." While she was glad that Abbie had steered the conversation away from her mortifying incident, this particular subject wasn't much easier. "I don't feel like I'm qualified for anything. I ran The Wagon Wheel for years, and even though Chuck's name was official first, I did the brunt of the work. I've got plenty of experience, but it seems to be the wrong kind on every job description I look at online. And don't get me started on trying to do it online in the first place!"

"That bad?"

Lori had picked up her laptop with the intention

of skimming through the job ads again, but she set it aside in disgust. Getting up, she walked across her small studio apartment into the kitchen. "It's just frustrating as hell. People don't always mark the position as being filled, so the same listings pop up even when they aren't available. I managed to get my apartment online, so I don't think it's me. I'm thinking about just going in person."

"Do people still do that anymore?"

Filling a glass of water, Lori shook her head. "I really don't know. It was how I got all my jobs in high school and college, though, and it's not like I'm having any luck trying to be modern about it."

"Then go for it!" Abbie encouraged. "The worst thing they're going to do is tell you no."

As she stepped out of her kitchen, Lori looked around at her apartment. It was just a tiny one-bedroom with few luxuries, yet it had cost her dearly. There was a significant difference between this little city and Chinook. Her savings had allowed her to get out there, but it wouldn't last much longer. "You're right. I think I'm going to get out there and do it."

Considering her work experience, Lori moved through the downtown area later that afternoon, checking in at every bar and restaurant she found. A few gave her applications to fill out and bring back, several told her they only took online applications, and plenty said they weren't hiring at all.

It was now dark and her feet were getting sore, but Lori continued on. There had to be someplace that was hiring. The applications she'd accumulated felt more like a way to get her to leave than anything else. She was just wondering what happened to the days of being hired on the spot when a deep, pulsing rumble caught her ears.

Looking across the street, Lori spotted a flat brick façade under the streetlights. It would've looked like nothing more than some old warehouse except for the curling white letters painted directly onto the brick to advertise Selene's. Judging by the loud music pumping out of the place, it had to be some sort of rock club. She read the names of the bands on a marquee that'd been put up over the plain black double doors. Bleak Future. Punctured. The She-Wolves. Lori had never heard of any of them, and the place looked nothing like the country saloon she was used to, but she was willing to try anything at this point.

The music nearly blasted her back out onto the sidewalk as soon as she opened the door. A live band was playing on a stage to the right, with a seething mass of people dancing in front of it. Tables were scattered around the edge of the room, which was done entirely in black. Squinting at a post as she walked past it, Lori saw that people had signed the walls with paint markers. *Jenny wuz here '93. Marcus sucks balls. The Wolfgangs rule!*

She made her way through the throng of people over to the bar. The man behind it looked up at her with intense blue eyes that were bright, even in the darkness of the club. "What do you want?"

Clearly, customer service skills weren't required to work at this place. "I was just wondering if you're hiring."

"What?" He narrowed those intense eyes.

She'd been polite and sweet all day, but it wouldn't do her any good here. "Are you hiring?"

Now he'd finally understood, but it didn't help. "No." He went back to drying glasses.

Her shoulders sagged. This had all been for nothing. Lori was just about to head back outside when the door behind the bartender opened. Her mouth fell open when she saw who stood there.

He was just as hot as she remembered, but it was strange to see him in this loud bar instead of the quiet, finished basement of a house on the edge of town somewhere. Every time she'd thought of him since they'd met the other day, she only imagined him when she'd first opened her eyes, looking down at her with concern.

"Rex."

He looked just as stunned. "Lori. What are you doing here?"

The bartender had stepped to the side and was looking back and forth at each of them. "She was looking for a job, but I told her we're not hiring."

Rex pursed his lips. "No, we're not."

"We'll be back in five!" the band's lead singer announced, making the audience groan. There was still plenty of noise in the club even without the band playing, but at least she no longer had to strain to be heard.

Lori thought she should leave. The bartender clearly didn't like her, and she wasn't entirely sure that Rex was happy to see her. She'd spent only half an hour with him, yet she felt obligated to talk to him now that they were face-to-face again. "No one else seems to be hiring, either," she explained. "I've been all over town."

Rex was studying her, his brows low and his big arms folded in front of her chest. "I doubt you'd really want to work in a place like this, anyway."

Now it was her turn to narrow her eyes. This guy

might have helped her, but he knew nothing about her. Granted, she wasn't sure this was the sort of place she wanted to work, but she felt the challenge from him and wanted to battle against it, nevertheless. "Actually, up until recently, I was the co-owner of a thriving saloon in Montana."

"Well, I'm sure a honky-tonk is a lot tamer than this place." He leaned those big arms on the bar, never breaking his gaze.

"I don't know about that. Loud music, bar fights, spilled beer, guys who get too drunk and need their keys wrestled away from them before they go and do something stupid?" Granted, most nights at The Wagon Wheel weren't that bad, but he didn't need to know that.

His face hardened, and for a moment, Lori thought he was going to kick her out. Instead, he straightened and gestured with his head. "Step into the office for a moment."

Her stomach jumped into her chest, did a high-five with her heart, and dropped back down again. Did that mean there was a chance? She didn't want to be hired out of pity, but she needed a job desperately enough that she wasn't sure she cared.

The office's interior was small, barely more than a closet behind the bar. He had a desk set up along one wall, with a computer monitor and a scattering of papers sitting on top of it. A filing cabinet sat in the corner. It could have been cluttered and miserable, but Lori found it surprisingly cozy. It felt completely separate from the rest of the world. The band had just been starting up again when they'd come in, but the sound was instantly taken to a dull thud as soon as she shut the door behind her. "Soundproofing?"

"It's a bit of a necessity in a place like this," he explained as he eased his bulk into a chair and gestured at the other one across from the filing cabinet. "While I prefer to know exactly what's happening around here, I still have phone calls to make. How's your head, by the way?"

"Oh." She reached up to touch the side of her scalp. "It's fine. A bit bruised, but that's it."

"Good." He nodded curtly. "Now, tell me why you're so desperate for a job that you'd walk all over town, checking in at every place you can, including a place like this."

"I told you. I'm new in town. I need a paycheck."

"You also need to be more careful in the park," he cracked.

"So maybe jogging isn't my strong suit, but I don't think I'll need to mark that down as a skill for any job I might be trying to get." The chair wasn't very comfortable, and Lori wondered if it was designed that way to intimidate whoever used it. Rex didn't look nearly as kind and gentle as he had the other day when she'd woken up on his couch. In fact, he looked more interested in scaring her out of there.

"Let's say a bartender position opened up," he theorized.

"You said there wasn't one," she reminded him.

Those deep blue eyes burned into hers. "Humor me. Let's say you're that bartender. You've got five people waiting for drinks, a couple waiting to pay their tab, and your supplies need to be refilled. How are you going to handle that?"

"Drinks come first, as long as the supplies are there. Then checks, then supplies. They'll all get their turn." She wanted to smile, but she could tell that wasn't what he was looking for. If he thought she'd be overwhelmed with a busy bar, he'd assessed her completely wrong.

Rex gave no indication as to what he thought about her answer. "Sometimes things get dirty around here."

"I'm not afraid of dirt. I raised a boy, after all. And I'm used to the dirt you're talking about." That was the one thing she liked least about working in a bar, but it was also the sort of thing that a person just got used to.

"Customers can be difficult. They don't like their drinks, or they want to fight," he fired back.

"Right. It's easy enough to ask them what they didn't like about it and remedy that. Fights happen, and every one is different. Usually, getting the aggressor's attention while someone else removes the other guy does the trick. You never go in alone." There had only been a handful of times she'd had to do this, as most people at The Wagon Wheel were fairly peaceful. There was a lot she'd learned in all her years there, though.

Still his face showed no emotion. "We work late nights, weekends, and holidays."

"Comes with the territory, and I'm used to the schedule." Lori folded her hands in her lap, hoping she looked relaxed even though she didn't feel like it. This guy was quite the character. He rescued her after hitting her head and was enough of a gentleman to drive her home, but right now, he looked like he could just as easily open his jaws and eat her.

They sat in silence for a moment that stretched into eternity. "I'm not hiring," he finally said.

"All right." She could challenge him on why he'd

wasted both of their time if he was going to be like that, but she didn't. Lori stood. "I'll get back to finding someplace that is, then."

"But I'm going to hire you," he continued as she reached for the doorknob.

Lori turned and studied him, waiting.

"I hadn't officially opened a position yet, which is why both Max and I told you that we weren't hiring. However, I've noticed a bit of a gap in the schedule, and we could use someone to help fill that in. It means you'll be at the bottom of the ladder, and you'll have the least control over when you work. The pay is decent, though, and our patrons usually tip generously as long as you treat them right."

Inside, she was throwing her arms around him, smacking her lips against his cheek, and thanking him a million times. Her job hunt had been so long and frustrating. Her eyes had gone dry from staring at online job listing sites, and now her feet were sore from schlepping all over town, so this was exactly what she needed. It didn't matter that this guy was kind of strange and that Selene's itself was a bit intimidating. It was a paycheck! Outside, though, she simply nodded. "When do I start?"

4

MUSIC THUDDED THROUGH HIS EARS AND INTO HIS soul. It made his wolf churn inside him, but at least it was in a way he was used to. That wasn't exactly what was happening every time his eyes darted across the room and found Lori.

Rex sat at a table in the back corner where he had a good vantage of the entirety of Selene's. His office was fine for booking bands, making schedules, entering payroll, and conducting pack business, but Rex recognized the importance of getting down to the meat and bones of the club to fully understand it.

Dark Love was onstage at the moment. They had a slower vibe than most of the thrashy, heavy, hard-core bands that he usually booked, but it was early in the evening. They were perfect for the crowd that had gotten off work and needed a place to unwind. His third in command, Dave, was behind the bar. He'd always enjoyed Selene's, and Rex suspected this was because it gave him access to so many women. The male patrons didn't always appreciate his attention, but they dealt with it. He was swift as he made drinks, wiped down the bar, and restocked the supplies.

Then there was Lori. She'd already had a turn behind the bar, and Rex knew it wasn't a mistake that Dave had invited her to step up just as the crowd got thicker. Rex himself had thought she might get rattled if she had to do more than pop the tops off a couple of beers or pour a whiskey, but she'd proven them wrong. She'd easily whipped up margaritas, whiskey sours, and mojitos. She hardly spilled a drop, but when she did, she took care of it quickly.

Right now, she was waiting tables. She made her rounds through the room, gathering orders from two groups at a time so she had a full tray by the time she returned. She was efficient, and Rex doubted anyone felt they'd waited too long. When she returned to the bar, Dave said something to her.

Rex's hearing was excellent despite his many

years running Selene's, and he knew he could thank his wolf blood for that. It wasn't sensitive enough to let him hear what the two of them were saying over the noise of the band, though. Dave pointed at several things behind the bar, his brows low and jaw tight. Rex pulled in a breath, waiting to see where this would go, but Lori just smiled, shrugged, and moved past him to make the White Russian someone had ordered.

He didn't have to wait long to find out what was happening because Dave came charging across the room at him a moment later. "What the fuck is wrong with you?"

Although Rex felt that any of the senior members of the pack should take their job seriously, Dave had a penchant for taking it to another level. It made it impossible not to bust his balls a little every now and then. "Lots. I made your whiny ass my third in command, for starts."

"Dick." Dave gripped the back of the empty chair next to Rex, not bothering to sit. His body was full of tense energy, radiating off him in thick waves. "You know what I'm talking about."

Again, it was just too easy. "And then I gave you a job here. What the hell was I thinking?"

"Damn it, Rex! This is your business we're

talking about, as well as your pack!" Now Dave did sit, if only to get his point across. "How could you hire her?"

Looking past Dave, Rex watched Lori now that she was pretty much running the place by herself. She did exactly as she'd said she would in her interview, making sure the customers who were still drinking were happy before she attended to anything else. "It was simple enough. I'd been thinking about opening up a position for a while. The schedule was a little bare as it was, and then if someone was sick or needed time off, we were fucked. I want my employees to get a good amount of hours, but I don't want them working so hard that they're miserable. You ought to be thanking me, not only for hiring her but for going ahead and doing it while we've got time to make sure she's trained. No one's requested any time off for the next couple of weeks, so it'll be low pressure."

"And the fact that she's human?" Dave pressed. "Doesn't that matter to you at all?"

Rex had known it would only be a matter of time before the issue was brought up, and he knew that timeframe would be a short one. Dave had already been pissed about having Lori at the packhouse when she was injured, and he definitely didn't like having her there at Selene's. "Not in the way you think it should," he replied calmly.

"She makes the shifters uncomfortable," Dave urged. "Not just the employees, but the guests, too. I can see it in their eyes every time she waits on them. They can tell she's a human, which is obvious from a mile away. They've always come here because they know this place is staffed by wolves. You're going to start losing customers once word gets out."

"Maybe," Rex replied slowly, "but it's not like this place has ever been strictly for shifters. We get humans in here all the time, yet the traffic doesn't slow down."

"It's different when we're talking about a worker," Dave insisted. "This has always been a safe place for people like *us* to work."

"And it still is." Rex was keeping his calm, although Dave was certainly challenging it. "Then there's the fact that she actually smiles at her customers while serving them and treats them with respect. That's more than I can say about you."

Dave tightened his lips and glanced at the stage. "Fine. If you don't think this is a problem for the customers or the staff, then think about the bands. They practically fight for a slot here because they know Selene's is run not only by a shifter but by an

Alpha. This is one of the most influential places where any band can play. What do you think will happen when they find out what you're doing here? You'll be begging them to play here instead of the other way around. This place will go straight down the shitter if you don't have the bands to hold it up."

Rex tapped his fingers thoughtfully on the table. While Dave's theories weren't completely impossible, they weren't likely. One person couldn't upend their entire pack and the Eugene music scene. "You were pretty bent out of shape when Lori was brought to the packhouse," he noted.

"Of course," Dave growled.

"And you thought she might be trying to spy on us." The accusations that'd flown from him in those moments had been ridiculous, but that didn't mean Rex wouldn't use them to their fullest advantage. "Then don't you think it would be good if I kept tabs on her?" Rex challenged. "Wouldn't it be far better to see her on a regular basis, to help her make sure she's got her bills paid, to know what's going on in her life instead of just waiting around to see if she figures us out?"

"You want to keep an eye on her by bringing her right into our midst?" Dave raked his fingers through his short dark hair, and his nearly black eyes flicked across the room to Lori. "I try to have respect for you and what you do, Rex, but that's downright stupid."

Rex's wolf shoved at the underside of his skin, demanding to be let out so he could let Dave know just what he thought of that accusation. "One could argue that the only person being stupid here is the one who is challenging his Alpha's authority. I've run this club and this pack for a long time, Dave. I learned from the best, and I know what I'm doing."

"I'm not so sure about that." Dave bared his teeth.

In one swift movement, Rex wrapped his fingers around Dave's forearm and pressed his thumb into the pressure point just below his elbow. "I am. I'm both the owner of this club and the Alpha, as you keep saying. Remember that, as well as your place. Go take a break. I think you could use some fresh air."

Dave's coal-black eyes flashed, but he gave a quick, stiff nod. Rex let go, and the other man strode out the side door without a word.

His adrenaline was up, and there was nothing Rex needed more right now than a quick run through the woods in his wolf form. It'd been too long since he'd let it out, something that didn't sit well with him. He'd always prided himself on running his pack in a more traditional way than many others did these days, so he'd have to remedy that soon. For the moment, he had a club to run.

The band didn't need anything from him, but Dave's impromptu break meant Lori was managing the bar alone. It was almost eight, which meant things were about to get crazy.

She glanced up as he stepped behind the bar, surprise in her velvety eyes. "Hey."

"How are things going?" Snagging a half-apron from a hook behind the bar, he quickly whipped it around his waist. "Do you have any questions about anything?"

A hint of a smile played on her lips. "I've been able to find my way around."

"Dave didn't show you where things were?" The lemon slices were getting low, so he grabbed a basket of them from the mini fridge under the bar.

"Um..." Lori flicked her hair out of her way, which she'd arranged in a loose French braid that highlighted all the different colors coming together in long, swirling streaks.

"You're not going to get him in trouble if that's what you're worried about. I know how Dave can be. You can consider it a test to see if I really should've hired you." He wanted to capture that braid in his hand, to feel the texture of it as it slid against his palm.

"So did I pass?" she asked as she reached past him to grab a glass.

The space was limited back there. She'd said she'd owned a saloon for a long time, so working in close quarters with someone would be nothing new or uncomfortable. It shouldn't be for him, either, but his body constantly measured the distance between them. His wolf had been eager to come out when Dave confronted him, but now it was lunging toward her. It'd had the same reaction when she'd been on the couch back at the packhouse, and he'd felt it all over again when she'd suddenly shown up at Selene's the day before. Fate was putting this woman in his way for a reason, but he had yet to figure out what it was. "Well enough," he grumbled.

"Most of it was fairly self-explanatory anyway," she continued as she grabbed a bottle from the shelf. Her hands moved with the confidence and expertise of someone who could make drinks without having to think about it.

Seeing that made Rex realize he'd never put her through the rigors of making him several drinks to test her bartending skills as he would for any other potential employee. So maybe there was some bias there, but that wasn't what Dave had been complaining about. "You said you had a place out in Montana for a long time. I know you said you came out here to be closer to your son, but a long-term steady business is hard to give up."

"Just a sec." With her drink finished, she quickly ran it out to the customer instead of making them wait while she chatted. "It was just one of those things that happens."

"Like the place closing down or something?" He finished with the first lemon and flicked the seeds into the trash before he grabbed another one. Her background shouldn't matter to him. He'd already hired her, after all, so what was the point in finding out? He couldn't help himself.

"Like running the place with my husband for most of our adult lives until he left town with the hostess," she replied as she dumped a bucket of ice from the machine into the bin below the bar.

His paring knife slipped, and he cursed under his breath as he nearly sliced through his finger.

"I don't think people will want your pinkie in their lemon drop."

"You never know. We've got a lot of weirdos around here." He wiped his hands off to make sure the mistake didn't happen again. "That's rough, though."

"Sure." Lori moved behind him to get to the sink on the other side of him, her hip brushing against his backside as she did. "It was a shock, but I guess it wasn't really a surprise."

In his mind's eye, he could easily see the horrified look on Lori's face as she realized what her husband had done. He could practically feel her pain in his heart, and he forced himself to focus on the damn lemons. If anything, he should be glad it happened. He had an experienced bartender to step in and help versus someone who needed full training. Human or not, there was no denying that Lori knew what she was doing.

But did she have any idea what she was doing to him?

5

"I MADE YOUR FAVORITE," LORI SAID AS SHE OPENED the door for Conner.

He stepped inside and looked around. "Looks like you still have quite a few boxes."

"Easy to say for someone who left home with little more than a duffel bag and a suitcase," she commented as she popped up on her tiptoes to kiss his cheek. He ducked back a little, as she expected him to, but that wasn't going to stop her. Conner might be a college linebacker topping six feet and over two hundred pounds, but he was still her little boy. "How is the dorm treating you?"

He rolled a big shoulder. "Fine, I guess."

Lori knew not to expect much more than that out of him. "Come on in and sit down. I feel like I've hardly seen you at all since I've been here. Do you want a Coke?"

"Water is fine." He pulled out a dining chair and sat, making the small table look tiny.

The real estate listing had claimed the apartment had a dining room, but it was really nothing more than a bit of space between the kitchen and living room that fit a table. Even so, Lori was grateful. It made the place feel a little more like home, and she hoped it would do the same for Conner.

"Here we are." She piled a plate high with a generous cut of pot roast, a heap of potatoes, and a scoop of carrots.

He frowned at the last part.

"Don't tell me you still don't like vegetables," she chided gently as she served up her own plate and joined him at the table. "You're an adult now. You have to start eating a little more responsibly."

"Yeah." He picked up his fork and stabbed a potato.

"I guess you probably hear the same thing from your coach."

"Mmhm." He focused on his meal without looking up.

"The roast is nice and tender. It felt so strange to cook in a new kitchen, and I wasn't sure how it

would all come out. It's a much smaller kitchen, too."
It was more efficient, considering it didn't take more
than two steps to get from one side of it to the other.
"I really have to keep up on the dishes, or they
instantly start looking like a mountain."

"I'm sure." He shoved a bite of roast in his
mouth.

Lori studied him from across the table. He'd
never been particularly talkative, but he'd started
getting even quieter over the last few years. It'd
started in high school, and Lori had been sure it was
simply a matter of adjusting to teenage life. She
didn't envy him; high school kids could be cruel.
He'd still been getting decent grades and keeping up
with football practice, so she hadn't been particularly worried. Now, she was starting to wonder.
Something was going on, and he wasn't telling her.
"Do you have a girlfriend, honey?"

This earned her a bit of a laugh as he scratched
the side of his nose with his thumb. "Uh, no."

"You know you can tell me if you do, right?"

"I just said I didn't, Mom."

"I know, but you're in college now. It's not like
you have to bring her over for dinner or get my
approval or anything." Not that she wouldn't absolutely love to meet a girl Conner was interested in,

but she didn't want him to start keeping secrets from her just because he thought she was going to get involved. "I want to be a part of your life, but I know you're also trying to find yourself."

"Mmph." He poked a carrot with his fork and stacked it with a small potato.

Lori took a breath. "I know the stuff that happened between your father and me must have been hard on you."

He shook his head. "It's fine, Mom."

"Is it?" She took a sip of her water, knowing it most definitely wasn't, at least for her. Time had made things easier, and she no longer felt the heartbreak racking her chest. Chuck had been a real ass, but she wouldn't let him keep her back. "I worry that I got so caught up in the divorce and selling The Wagon Wheel that you and I haven't really had a chance to talk about it all."

Conner finally looked up at her. "Mom, don't worry about it. I know what Dad did. He's a shithead. I still talk to him every now and then because he's my dad, but it's not like I'm suffering some great trauma from it all. I'm not a little kid, and I was about to move out when it all went down anyway."

"Okay, but I worry that I didn't discuss all the right things with you before you left because I was so busy. I mean, college provides a lot of opportunities, but not always for good things. I don't want you to be unprepared for the world if, say, you want to get intimate with a girl."

"Mom."

"I know. We had the talk when you were much younger, but there's a lot to cover. I'm still here to help. I was never able to talk to my mom about sex because she was so conservative about these things."

"Mom! Jesus!" Conner put his fork down next to his plate. "I said there wasn't a girl! And before you ask, no guys, either."

"What about—"

"No drugs. No alcohol. Nothing you could make a public service announcement about." Conner grabbed his fork again and resumed eating.

Damn. She was just trying to be open and honest, unlike her parents had been. They'd buried their heads in the sand, preferring to pretend that sex didn't exist and that babies were still delivered by a freaking stork. If it hadn't been for magazines, her friends, and the once-a-year sex ed class, she wouldn't have known a damn thing.

"So, how are things going with football?" Surely that would be a safe thing to ask.

He shrugged, his favorite gesture. "Fine." His favorite word.

"I'd imagine it gave you some instant friends once you moved here. I mean, you certainly have something in common." Was her apartment always this quiet, or had she just not sat still long enough to notice?

"Sort of. We get along fine at practice and during games and everything. I just..." He paused, his forkful of potatoes halfway to his mouth. "I feel different from everyone here."

"I can understand that." Finally, something more than a one-word sentence! "Eugene is a far cry from Chinook, or anywhere else in Montana for that matter. I wish I knew exactly how to describe it, but I know what you mean."

"That's good because I don't have a clue how to explain it."

"My accent gave me away immediately," she said, recalling that Rex had mentioned it. "I don't even think of myself as having an accent, but I guess I do."

He laughed a little. "Yeah, you do."

Feeling like she was on a role, Lori kept going. "And everyone here seems to really be into working out. I see them out jogging or hiking all the time, even in the middle of winter. I've driven by more juice bars and smoothie places than I can count."

"That's not so bad."

She felt her stomach muscles relax a bit. They might not be waxing philosophical on the problems of modern society, but at least they were having a conversation again. "I figured it was about time I started thinking about that myself, honestly. I even got myself one of these."

Conner looked up as she pulled back her sleeve. "You're the last person I'd expect to have a fitness tracker."

"Thanks a lot." She slapped his arm. "It doesn't even seem to work that well. I don't think it's accurately tracking all of my steps, and I swear it thought I was dead yesterday. It didn't register my heart rate at all."

"You're wearing it too loose." He reached across the table and adjusted the band. "You don't want it to cut your circulation off or anything, but it won't get accurate information if it's too floppy."

Surprised that he would offer to adjust the band himself, Lori looked up at her son. "How do you know?"

He pulled back his sleeve to reveal the fitness tracker on his wrist and smiled. "Coach recommended them so we can start paying attention to our ideal heart rate for calorie burning and building stamina. I didn't think I'd like it at first, but it's kind of cool."

It felt so good to finally see him smile. Even if it was just for something minor, it let Lori know that Conner had found some happiness out there. He didn't want her to worry about him or fuss over him, but he had no idea just how difficult that was.

"Are you ready for some brownies?"

"You made brownies, too?" he asked as he dragged his fork across his plate to gather up any scraps that hadn't made it into his mouth yet.

"Just from a mix, anyway. I've been working a lot of hours, so I haven't had much time." Lori took her plate into the kitchen.

Conner followed her with his own and rinsed them both in the sink while she took the cover off the brownie pan. "What's the place like?"

Her knife sliced easily down into the thick brownies. "Well, it's a rock club."

He turned around and raised his dark blonde eyebrows. "Really? I guess you're doing all sorts of things that don't seem like you."

"Maybe I'm finally finding out who I really am," she shot back.

He accepted the dessert plate, but he was watching her closely. "I think I can relate to that."

"I mean, I was just a wife and mother for over twenty years," she went on as she cut a brownie for herself. Hell, if she was going to cheat on this whole heart-healthy thing, she might as well go all the way. "I was more concerned about paying the bills and wiping your nose than figuring out what I really liked or wanted. Not that I would trade a single second of it," she added.

"So, what's the name of this rock club?" He fished a new fork out of the drawer.

"Selene's. It's kind of a hole in the wall from the outside, nothing that looks all that notable, but they do a lot of business. What? Why are you looking at me like that?" Lori licked the side of her mouth, figuring she had a bit of frosting she'd missed.

Conner was staring at her hard. "It's just... I heard that's kind of a rough place."

So that was it. He was worried about his mother. Well, she'd take it. Lori knew that worry came from love. "It's not that bad, really. I don't think it's much different from The Wagon Wheel. Of course, you have to swap out cowboy boots for combat boots, and there sure isn't any line dancing going on, but it's still just a bunch of people getting together to listen to music. And actually, it turns out I know the guy who owns the place."

"You do?" He nearly choked on his brownie but quickly recovered. "How can you know anyone but me when you just moved here?"

"It's not like I just sit in this apartment all day alone. Sometimes I go out jogging to pretend like I fit in, and I whack my head so I can be revived by strangers and make new friends," she replied with a grin. "It's the guy I told you about that brought me home that day."

A look of horror flashed across his face. "Is this like... a thing?"

Something lurched inside her at the mere thought. It *wasn't* a thing, just one of those weird circumstances that life throws at you sometimes. She hadn't known anyone in Eugene, but she did now. And that connection, she was sure, had helped her secure the job she needed so badly. Simple, except for that goose egg on her head.

And the charge of energy that flowed through her every time Rex looked at her with those sapphire eyes.

She'd expected him to be holed up in his office most of the time, but he got his hands dirty just like the rest of them. Whatever needed to happen, he made sure it did. Rex served drinks, swept the floor, and even helped the bands haul their equipment out to their vans at the end of the night when the lights came on.

"No," she said, realizing she'd taken far too long to answer the question. "No, it's not a thing. I just work for him."

Conner tipped his head and did his best impression of a parental figure. "Because you know, if you were interested in getting intimate with this man, we might need to sit down and talk about birth control."

"Stop it!" she laughed as she gave him another playful slap on the arm. "Unless you actually want me to start talking about the birds and the bees. I'm sure I can find some enlightening materials on the subject down at the library."

"Okay, okay! I give up. Truce! I don't want to know!" He put his hands in the air, one of them still holding his plate.

They laughed some more as they finished cleaning up, and before she knew it, it was time for Conner to head back to his dorm. "Thanks for dinner, Mom. Let me know if you need more help moving furniture, boxes, or anything."

"I will. Bye, honey. I love you." When she closed the door behind him, she let out a long sigh.

Lori made her way back into the living room. She picked up the TV remote, but she didn't turn it on. This visit with Conner should've made her so happy. She'd come to Eugene for the sole purpose of being closer to him, and he'd spent almost two hours at her place. They'd eaten together, and they'd even managed to laugh a little.

But she couldn't shake the feeling that he was holding something back. Lori knew he wasn't a child anymore, and he certainly had no obligation to tell her about every detail of his life. Hell, she probably didn't even want to know. But she'd seen that look in his eyes. It was the same one he had when he'd failed a big test in school and didn't want to have to come forward about it or when he and his friends had been caught toilet papering a neighbor's yard at Halloween. Those were minor things in the long run, but they'd been huge to him at the time.

What could be that big now?

6

"I HOPE THIS IS IMPORTANT. I'VE GOT A LOT TO TAKE care of." Rex stepped into the basement and looked around at his family, who all waited for him expectantly.

"Of course you do," his father said. Jimmy and Joan Glenwood were seated together on the loveseat. Jimmy held his mate's hand, their wrinkled fingers intertwined. "There's always a lot on any Alpha's plate."

"We understand that very well," his mother intoned in her smoky voice. She brushed her curly gray hair back, revealing a long, shimmering earring. "It can be a difficult burden to bear, but that doesn't mean you have to do it alone. It also doesn't say anything negative about you if you need to ask for help. In fact, one of the signs of a great leader is someone who knows when to reach out."

Rex lowered himself into an armchair, feeling impatient. "What is this? An intervention?"

His brother Brody laughed, but he didn't look up from his sketchpad. "You could call it that."

"I serve plenty of alcohol, but I hardly ever touch the stuff. I don't have any vices, unless you think I watch too many band videos online. That's just the nature of my work," Rex explained. In fact, that was probably what he needed to be doing right now. He had the club booked straight through the next month, but after that was a little spotty. Holes needed to be filled, which wouldn't happen overnight. Sure, bands would be banging his door down if he opened it up on a first-come, first-served basis, but then he'd be allowing complete trash to take the stage. He'd built a reputation for Selene's, and he wasn't going to flush it down the toilet.

"The nature of *that side* of your work," Joan corrected gently. "This is about pack business."

Rex knitted his brows together as he studied his mother. "What are you talking about?"

Jimmy finally let go of his mate's hand and sat forward, bracing his elbows on his knees and steepling his fingers together. "Some other pack members have come to us with concerns about the human woman."

Anger boiled up inside of him. Though Rex wasn't upset with his father for talking to him about this, he didn't know why the hell anyone thought there was a reason to complain. "I've got everything under control."

"They don't seem to think so." Dawn was standing near the fireplace. She was still dressed in her scrubs and had her greying hair tied back in a messy bun, suggesting that she'd come straight from work. Or had the family called her out there early? "I've had several of them ask if I'm sure I erased her memory of seeing the pack shift."

"And what did you tell them?" Rex understood what an uncomfortable position that put Dawn in. She'd used her tincture and performed her spell, but she'd left the rest up to Rex.

She gave a little shrug. "What could I tell them other than the truth? I didn't talk to her, so I don't know. But I explained that you had and that you were satisfied."

"Which should've been all the reassurance anyone would need," Rex affirmed. His wolf reminded him that he never had gone out for that run. He'd been too damn busy. He'd have to make time soon, though. The irritation of this impromptu meeting was getting under his skin, but there was no room for it. His wolf already occupied the space.

"You'd think so, but apparently, it wasn't." Brody tipped his head to the side and then rotated his sketchbook before he continued drawing, the creases at the corners of his eyes becoming more prominent as he concentrated on his work. "I've had a few asking me about it, too. I told them I didn't know a damn thing about it. I was at the shop all day when that happened."

"So you just shrugged it off?" Rex growled. Brody could be laid back to a fault. He was constantly either drawing on paper or tattooing his designs into people, and little else grabbed his attention. "You should've told them I'd taken care of it."

"I did." Brody's hazel eyes, the same color as Dawn's and their mother's, flicked up to him for a brief moment before returning to his art. "Just like Dawn said, it wasn't enough."

"We've all had pretty much the same experiences," Joan said. "That's why we're here, and that's why it's just the family. We need to address this before we get the rest of the pack involved.

Rex's eyes swiveled over to the couch, the same couch where Lori had lain as she came back to the conscious world after that whack to the head. Max sat there now, looking dark and brooding as usual. "What about you? Did anyone say anything to you?"

The Glenwood pack's beta sat silent for a moment, the muscles in his jaw working back and forth, highlighting the touch of silver in his stubble. He was the quiet one of the bunch, and Rex wasn't sure he would say anything at all. "At work," he finally said. "No one's happy about having a human on the staff."

Rex threw his hands in the air. "Is this all from Dave? Because he's already talked to me about this, and I put him in his place. He doesn't run the pack, nor does he run the club. I'm fully justified in everything I've done, and I shouldn't have to explain that over and over again."

Jimmy scratched his head of gray hair, which had once been as dark as Dawn's and Max's. "Why don't you tell us a little more about things from your perspective?"

He pressed his tongue against the back of his teeth. It wasn't an unreasonable request, but he was having a hard time letting go of the indignation he felt at being questioned. It was his damn pack, after all. "Fine. Some of the guys were out in the woods behind the packhouse, and Lori saw them shift. She ran off, but she tripped and hit her head. They brought her back here because they didn't know what to do with her. Dawn erased her memory of the event, and I took her home."

"Simple enough," Jimmy said with a nod.

"Except that Dave thought we should kill her," Dawn chimed in. "That's actually why I didn't stick around to see that the spell worked. I figured he'd want to bitch about it a bit more, but he was gone when I went upstairs."

Yet another ripple of exasperation moved along Rex's skin. Dave was the Glenwood pack's third in command. It was his role to protect the pack from any outside threats that he perceived, but he should've trusted Rex that Lori wasn't a threat at all.

"Then Lori showed up at Selene's," Rex continued, figuring he needed to just get all of this out in the open. "She's new in town, and she was looking for a job. I went ahead and hired her. It was the perfect opportunity to keep an eye on her and make sure that she hadn't seen anything she wasn't supposed to while she was here."

"Is she hot?" Brody asked as he set down one pencil and picked up another.

"What?" Rex barked.

His brother shrugged and grinned. "Just asking.

You wouldn't be the first guy to hire a woman just because she had nice jugs or something."

Dawn made a disgusted noise. "For fuck's sake!"

"Just being honest," Brody argued.

"I don't think any of this is the point," Max said. "Selene's has always been run by us. Now we've got a human in the mix just because she was clumsy enough to trip and hit her head?"

Rex's fists balled on the arms of his chair, but he forced them to relax. Lori wasn't clumsy, but if he jumped to her defense, it would only prove to his accusers that he'd hired her for all the wrong reasons. "As I told Dave, we have plenty of humans who come to the club. It's not like I can keep them out. Hell, even some have been in the bands I hire. So I might be thwarting a little tradition by putting her on the payroll, but that's my prerogative. Besides, she's one hell of a bartender. She can mix drinks blindfolded, and more importantly, the customers like her."

And if he were completely honest with himself, he liked her, too. He liked the way she had a genuine smile on her face when she greeted a patron or delivered their drink to them. He liked that happy energy that came off her when someone told her they liked what she'd made. Lori wasn't just doing a job to get a paycheck. She actually cared about what she was doing. He'd be hard-pressed to find someone else like that in the service industry, human or otherwise.

"You know, back in our day, we liked to take as democratic of an approach as possible," Jimmy noted, leaning back.

Here we go. Yes, his father had been Alpha for a long time before him, and he certainly had plenty of experience leading their pack. There was a reason that he'd stayed in charge long enough to retire, passing his title down to Rex. Still, listening to him wax nostalgic about the good ol' days wasn't exactly prime entertainment.

"We wanted to make sure not only that we were leading," the older man continued, "but that we were doing the kinds of things the other members were willing to follow. There's a fine balance between doing what's best for the pack and what the pack *thinks* is best for them. We tried to get as much input from the other members as possible, but we also explained why we made the decisions we did."

"That was the same way we raised you kids," Joan added, letting out a throaty laugh. "I guess one task isn't really all that different from the other, when you think about it."

Jimmy smiled at his mate before turning back to

Rex. "I guess I'm saying that you might want to get everyone else a little more involved. A unilateral stance is certainly very traditional, and we've kept a lot of the traditional ways here, but it's not always appreciated."

"Dave says you won't listen to reason," Dawn explained with a regretful look. "He doesn't understand why there's any reason to keep this woman around if, as you say, her memory erasure was successful."

Rex's throat tightened. Was there a reason, or was he just fooling himself so that he could keep her within his own reach? Though he never would've admitted it out loud, there was some sort of connection between himself and Lori. He felt it, and more importantly, his wolf did whenever she was around. Her very soul reached out and touched his. Rex didn't know how to reject those touches, and he wasn't sure he wanted to.

Explaining all of that would only make his family doubt him more. It would also feel like admitting defeat. "I think everyone is taking this too far. Having her under my observation for the moment doesn't mean any of this is permanent. I can fire her tomorrow if I decide to. It's not like I'm inviting her to the packhouse for a meeting or anything."

"I could always pull some cards and see what the divine has to say about this woman's impact on us," Joan suggested. "We've all found that to be a tremendous source of guidance."

"No offense, Mom, but I don't think tarot cards are the solution here." Rex had full respect for the magical abilities on his mother's side. Her home pack had also been a coven of witches, an unusual yet powerful combination. There were indeed many times that those skills had aided the pack. Right now, though, Rex wasn't interested in finding out what they had to say about Lori. He knew enough about her on his own to be satisfied with her presence at Selene's.

"Don't you have some friends who own other bars and clubs around Eugene? Ones that are a little more lax about who they hire?" Brody asked as he reached for an eraser. "You could just have one of them hire her for a slightly better pay rate or something. That would be one way of getting rid of her if you don't want to fire her."

"Why should it matter if he fires her?" Max asked. "It would be swift and quick."

"Who says she even has to be a bartender?" Dawn stepped away from the fireplace. "There are plenty of positions open at the hospital, and humans are all over the place. She'll fit right in."

"I suppose I didn't make myself clear." Rex put his hands on his knees and stood, looking around at his family. He knew they all cared about him, and he loved them just as much. But they were still family, which meant they could be a royal pain in the ass at times. "This isn't about giving her a job. Yes, that's worked out for me, but that wasn't the point. It's about whether or not she poses a security risk. I've already established that while I don't believe she does, I'm going to keep her on my radar until I know for sure. It's all straightforward, and it's all been taken care of. I appreciate your suggestions and concerns, but I've got this. The rest of the pack needs to understand that there will just be some things that aren't up to them."

He looked around, waiting for one of them to continue arguing with him. They only sat silently, watching.

"Now, if we're done here, I've got more important things to do than sit around and debate what those important things are and how I should be doing them. Excuse me." He turned and headed back up the stairs.

Once in his den, he locked the door for good

measure. The last thing he needed was for his mother to come waltzing in there in her flowy outfit to ask if he was all right and if he wanted her opinion. He sat behind his computer and pulled up the scheduling spreadsheet he'd been working on when Dawn had summoned him. Sometimes it was easy to work from home, but apparently, not today.

Lori's name was right there on the left, taunting him from the schedule. *Lori Jensen.* He'd never even heard the name until a week ago, and now it was causing him more trouble than he'd ever imagined. For his peace of mind, he scanned over the shifts he'd scheduled her for. All total shit, just like he'd promised her they would be. Then he checked her total number of hours. He hadn't given her any advantages, and her pay was even a little lower than the starting wage he offered his pack mates. That meeting with his family had been a complete waste of time.

He was just about to switch over to the band schedule on another spreadsheet when he saw his own name. A long time ago, Rex had learned it made sense to arrange specific shifts for himself just like any other employee. It kept him from staying at the club too long or getting burned out. The staff seemed to like that when they saw the weekly schedule, too. It let them know he was just like them.

But the difference he did see was in the particular shifts he'd chosen. Rex had thought they were purely accidental, a result of working around his pack commitments and when his other workers were available. So why did so much of his time at Selene's coincide with Lori's?

No. There was nothing to it, and anyone who wanted to give him hell over who he hired could just get over it.

Even so, he scrapped the schedule and started a new one.

7

"No. Definitely not." Lori looked in the mirror at the new workout clothes she'd bought and laughed. "That's what I get for not trying things on at the store."

"Let me see!" Abbie said over the phone. "Put it on video!"

"Umm, no," Lori said as she struggled out of the spandex and back into her sweats. She tossed the leggings onto the bed and hoped she'd remember to return them later in the week.

Abbie laughed again. "Are they really that bad?"

"I learned quite some time ago how to dress these curves, and that ain't it!" Grabbing one of her favorite t-shirts from the closet and throwing it over her head, Lori sat down to put on her shoes.

"You're really into this whole fitness thing, aren't you?"

She shrugged, even though she knew Abbie couldn't see her from two states away. "According to my doctor, I don't have much choice unless I'm willing to live with these perimenopause symptoms. I don't exactly love mood swings that take me from zero to sixty or tossing and turning in sweaty sheets all night. I've gotta say, it's been helping my sleep a little already. Conner showed me a few things about this fitness tracker, so it's actually working now."

"Aw, that's sweet of him."

"Yeah." Lori finished her double knot and straightened. She frowned as she thought about Conner.

"What is it?" Abbie always knew when something was wrong.

Lori stepped into the bathroom. She used her conditioning spray to keep her natural waves from getting frizzy and then pulled the whole mass into a ponytail. "I don't really know. Maybe it's nothing at all. I'm probably just worrying about him too much, but I felt like something was wrong when he was over here the other night for dinner."

"Wrong, how?"

Her ponytail was uneven, so she bent over and

tried again. "It was like he had something he wanted to tell me, but he didn't know how. That's pretty presumptuous, I know, and of course, he's a college kid. He doesn't want me to know everything. That's fine, but I want to be able to help if I can."

"Conner has always been a pretty good kid. I'm sure if something were truly wrong, something big, then he'd come to you," Abbie reassured her.

"I sure hope you're right." Lori fastened her elastic band, satisfied with her ponytail this time, and headed for the front door. "I'm sure this jog will do me some good. I need to let all these crazy thoughts blow out of my head and into the wind. I'll talk to you later, okay?"

"Sure thing. Bye!"

Lori stepped out the door. She'd found that the sidewalks near her apartment were just as suitable for a jog as that beautiful park was. The park hadn't exactly ended well, even though it'd probably played a role in her getting her job at Selene's. Lori felt comfortable sticking to the suburbs, and there were plenty of people around if she did something embarrassing again.

Lifting her wrist, Lori tapped the screen on her fitness tracker to let it know she was going for a jog. Big green letters flashed. GO! Well, the enthusiasm was nice, but she wasn't exactly going to take off like a jet.

She started off at a brisk walk to warm up. Her comment to Abbie about letting the wind blow her thoughts out of her mind certainly applied to Conner, but it also did to Rex. Lori hadn't been able to stop thinking about him ever since that day she'd wound up on his couch. Seeing him again at Selene's made her feel like she'd conjured him up herself. And now she worked for the man!

Lori picked up the pace a little into a slow trot. Did Rex have any idea just how difficult it was to work with him? Considering the dour face he usually wore, probably not. By all appearances, he just came in and did whatever the club needed. Nothing else mattered.

But she couldn't ignore the way he made her feel when she ended up working side by side with him. Her heart started pumping, and it wasn't because of the exercise. Lori couldn't remember the last time she'd felt so charged up about a guy, and it wasn't like he was even trying. The only thing he did seem to be trying to do was to keep his distance from her. If she stepped behind the bar, he went to check on the band. If he came into the stock room for supplies, he grabbed what he needed and hightailed it out of there without making any chitchat.

Selene's wasn't a big place, though, and they could only stay away from each other for so long. On the busier nights, they'd inevitably end up in the cramped space behind the bar, reaching past each other, accidentally brushing a hip or an arm. She'd reached for the high-end whiskey at the same time he had. Rex was faster, and her fingertips had brushed the backs of his. Lori had immediately jerked her hand back and mumbled an apology, but she hadn't missed the sparks that'd flown through her veins. Rex thrust the bottle at her a minute later with an impatient look.

Lori wondered just how much of this jog she would spend daydreaming about Rex. It was ridiculous! She was a grown woman, and he was her boss. He barely tolerated her, which was more than she could say for the other staff at the club. Max stayed away and didn't say a word, but at least that seemed to be his general attitude toward everyone. The others weren't any better. There were no friendly introductions or invites to do something outside of work. Not a soul had offered to give her tips about how the place ran unless she messed something up. The latter would earn her a sneer and a sigh as someone else fixed what they perceived to be a problem.

Given all of that, she supposed Rex was treating her pretty kindly.

Lori lifted her head and looked around her. Most of the buildings were more modern than she preferred, but she couldn't deny that everything seemed clean and cozy. The selection of businesses was remarkable compared to what she'd left behind in Chinook. She could get everything from home-made vegan burgers to Vietnamese spring rolls to Ethiopian injera and stews, none of which she'd ever had the opportunity to try. The people out on the sidewalks looked relaxed and happy as they moved from one place to another and met up with friends.

She felt her shoulders begin to relax as she started to get a bit more comfortable. It had felt so strange to move away from the only town she'd ever known. Back in Chinook, she wouldn't have been able to get out of her own driveway without seeing someone she'd known for years. People would stop to catch up in the supermarket or the post office. Football and basketball games were practically class reunions as the kids' parents visited in the bleachers. That was the kind of town Lori had been happy to grow up in and even happier to raise her son in.

Until everything happened with Chuck, anyway. People picked sides, and not all of them were on hers. They talked about her behind her back. Some were just feeling sorry for her, but it wasn't like she didn't know she was the subject of their conversations. With no family there to support her, Lori had found out quickly enough that even though she'd put her whole heart and soul into that town, the favor hadn't been returned.

She drew in a deep breath of relief, knowing she could leave it all behind here. Lori turned south, then west, to make a loop that would bring her back to her apartment.

"Lori."

Her heart had already been going at a steady pace from jogging, but it jumped just as badly as she did when a figure stepped out from the shadow of a building. Her fitness tracker beeped at her in alarm, and she slapped at the screen to get it to shut up.

"Dave. How nice to see you." She forced a smile and stepped to the left, ready to move around him and continue on.

He stepped directly in front of her, forcing her to stop completely. "We need to talk."

"Kind of in the middle of a workout here," she pointed out. Lori could use a break and was ready to slow back down to a walk. If anyone else had wanted to chat, she would've gladly stopped, but Dave wasn't anyone she particularly wanted to spend time with.

If he heard her, he didn't care. "I want you to stay out of Selene's."

Her guts curled up inside her when she looked into those dark eyes. She'd always thought their near-black color was due to the dim lights at Selene's. It turned out she was wrong. "It's my job, Dave. It's not like I can just work from home."

"Then quit." The consonants were so harsh on his tongue, they made her ears hurt. "No one wants you there. You already know that, so there's no point in trying to fool yourself any longer."

"Fine with me," she shrugged. "I'm not there to make friends."

A deep growl emanated from his throat. "Do you think this is funny? Maybe I should be a bit clearer. People like you aren't welcome at Selene's. If you keep coming back, you won't like the consequences."

Lori was used to dealing with drunks looking to get rowdy. She understood that remaining calm on the outside was the best tactic. If they could get you to crack, they'd pry it the rest of the way open just for fun. Dave, however, was perfectly sober and dead serious. There was no telling just what he might do, and what was she going to do about it? There were a few people out there on the street, but they weren't paying specific attention to her. Dave could grab her by the arm and drag her off without anyone noticing.

Still, she wasn't going to just lie down and give up. "I don't care what you or anyone else thinks about me, Dave. I have my job because I'm good at it, and I'm not going to quit just because I bother you for some strange reason. Go find someone else to intimidate because it won't work on me. I'm too old for this shit."

"I mean it," he snarled. "You ought to be lucky that I'm giving you a warning, and that's only for Rex's sake."

Fear had been creeping up her spine this whole time, but now it flooded her. Could he tell? Was she controlling her body well enough? People in the movies always talked about smelling fear, but she didn't know if that was really a thing. If Dave knew just what terror he was instilling in her right now, he'd be happier than a pig in shit.

For that very reason, she forced her right foot to lift up and step to the side. "Kiss my ass," she said as she breezed past him, quickly picking back up her jogging pace from before. It was easy enough, considering the adrenaline pumping through her system. She was glad she could work it all out without looking like she was running away from him. He didn't need to know that she was jogging far faster than she normally would.

She resisted the urge to turn around as she reached the end of the block to see if he was still there. Lori didn't need to, though. She could feel his gaze on her, making her skin crawl and her muscles tense. It was no coincidence that he was there right as she'd come through. He'd been waiting for her. Lori's stomach rolled again at the realization. That meant he'd probably been watching her the last time she took this route, and he'd even known when she stepped out her door.

A job at a rock club shouldn't be worth all of this, but she needed a steady paycheck. And then, of course, there was Rex.

She had to wonder, though, what Dave had meant when he said he'd given her a warning for Rex's sake. Did Rex know that Dave wanted her out? Of course he did, she realized. He had eyes in his head, and everyone in Selene's could see that Lori was the outcast. So had Rex specifically asked Dave to give her a warning? She wasn't sure how to feel about that.

Lori got back to her apartment in record time. She locked the door immediately behind her and closed the curtains. Because that creepy tingle wouldn't stop dancing up and down her spine, she checked under the bed and behind the shower curtain, just in case. If he'd stalked her on her jog and threatened her, there was no telling what he might be capable of.

When everything seemed as safe as it was going to get, Lori took out her cell phone and pulled up the number for the local police. She went through the conversation in her mind while she listened to the line ring. Lori didn't know Dave's last name, only where he worked. He'd said she wouldn't like the consequences if she continued to show up at Selene's, but was that enough of a threat for the cops to do anything?

Slowly, Lori put the phone away. Anything drastic was probably going to cost her job anyway. It would be easier to just wait and see how she felt about it tomorrow. Maybe she could talk to Rex about it. Maybe.

8

"MA'AM?"

Lori spotted the woman with her hand in the air and walked over, concerned when she saw that her drink was still full. "What can I do for you?"

The customer was a young woman, probably in her mid-twenties. Her lime green hair was bright even in the darkness of Selene's. "This isn't what I ordered."

"It's not? I'm so sorry." Lori reached for the rocks glass, feeling her stomach sink into her shoes. She hadn't been there long enough to mess up and feel okay about it. Rex had made it clear when he'd hired her that she'd be on probation for a while, and he could let her go at any time. It'd seemed a bit harsh, and she didn't think he'd really do it, but now she wasn't so sure.

The customer put her hand over the glass to keep Lori from taking it. "It's not what I ordered, but it's really good. It's like a whiskey sour, but better."

"Oh." Realization dawned on her as she understood what she'd done. "There's a drink we made back at the saloon I used to work at called the barrelman. It's a variation on a whiskey sour, but I've made so many of them that I must've just gone on autopilot. Would you like a regular whiskey sour? On the house." More like out of her paycheck, but that was fine. She'd take a hit for a few bucks if it meant she got to keep her job.

"No, that's okay," she said with a shake of her green hair. "Just tell me what a barrelman is."

Lori laughed, a sound that reverberated through the place. It was oddly quiet at the moment. "It's got a little extra bourbon and a bit of triple sec. An actual barrelman is the guy who distracts the bull during a bull riding competition. A rodeo clown. The joke at the saloon was that you'd need one of these drinks before you were brave enough to jump in the arena."

Laughing, the woman lifted her glass. "Sounds like just what I need!"

Relieved that things weren't nearly as bad as they'd seemed, or even bad at all, Lori returned to her place behind the bar.

"You got lucky with that one," Rex growled as he checked the stock of cold beers.

She'd already seen him do that at least twice that night, even though there was more than enough of it. "I know, but I like to think I make good drinks, even if they're the wrong ones."

His only response was a low grunt as he wiped down the bar, something else that didn't really need to be done.

Lori looked at him. "What's wrong?"

"Why would you think anything is wrong?" That earned her a flash of those bright blue eyes, but only for an instant.

She gestured vaguely at the club around them. "Well, you've been a grump all night. I mean, you're always grumpy, but it's worse than usual."

"Thanks for bringing that to my attention," he muttered.

"I'm just being honest." Lori knew she probably wouldn't have said that if this were any other job with any other boss. But she'd never met a moodier crowd than the staff at Selene's. "I know you sent everyone else home because it was a slow night, but maybe you should've just gone home yourself if it's that bad. I could've closed with someone else."

Again, those blue eyes blazed into hers. "No."

Something happened inside her when he looked at her like that. It should have been intimidating and uncomfortable, but it wasn't. It had, however, kept her from asking him more about Dave. She figured Rex was in a sour enough mood that he'd probably just blow her off if she brought it up. He'd known Dave a lot longer than he'd known her. Besides, the guy was an asshole, but Lori doubted Dave would actually follow through with his threats.

"Fine," she relented. "Be that way."

The last few customers paid their tabs and headed out the door, so Lori and Rex began the process of closing up. It was similar to what she'd always done at The Wagon Wheel, and she hardly had to think as she stepped out to wipe down all the tables. "It is because that band canceled?"

When he'd locked the door, he passed behind her, easily lifting the chairs and putting them upside down on the tables. "That's a big part of it."

"Doesn't that sometimes happen, though?" Lori challenged. "People get sick or have car trouble or whatever."

"It's nice to assume things are okay and that one

night doesn't matter, but it doesn't work like that. And it definitely doesn't work like that in this situation." He practically slammed the next chair onto the table. "They canceled because they decided they didn't want to play here anymore."

Lori stopped her efforts at cleaning the tables and put a hand on her hip. "Why would they go and do a thing like that? I don't know much about the rock scene, but I know that this is a really popular place for people to play."

His nostrils flared as he took a deep breath, and he turned away from her to get the next chair. "They had a problem with me."

"With your sparkling personality and stunning conversation? I don't see why," she replied dryly.

Now he stopped, his knuckles turning white as he gripped the back of a chair. "What the hell is that supposed to mean?"

For a brief moment, Lori wondered what was wrong with her. If she'd seen a man talking and acting the way Rex was right now, she'd be worried about what he might do next. With Rex, she felt completely different. "I'm just playing with you," she said with a smile. "You had a rough night, and I thought I might be able to make you laugh."

"Yeah. Good luck with that."

"There's nothing I can do to put you in a better mood?" she challenged.

This time when his eyes met hers, they held her steadily. "I can think of something."

Heat immediately began to burn under her skin, and it wasn't a hot flash. Lori could feel her body tingling in ways that it hadn't for a man in a long time. She turned away as she went to the next table. What the hell was that all about? He was her *boss*. He couldn't say things like that, and she sure as shit shouldn't be enjoying them.

"Your watch is flashing," his low voice said from behind her.

Sweeping her hand up to her face, Lori checked her fitness tracker. It was letting her know that her heart rate had increased. Great. Not embarrassing at all. She poked at the screen to get it to turn off.

Even though Conner had shown her some of the basics about this gadget, Lori realized she still had a lot to learn. She tapped and then tapped again, but the flashing continued. It went from yellow to green.

"Accessibility mode," the tracker announced aloud. "Your heart rate is one hundred thirty beats per minute. You're in the prime fat-burning zone. Great job!"

"No!" Lori could feel her heart rate continue to

skyrocket as her fingers pecked feverishly at the stupid thing. Of course her heart rate was going up, and it would only keep heading in that direction as long as the tracker was announcing it.

"Keep going!" it cheered. "You're achieving your goals!"

Sure, if her goal was to let Rex know exactly what he did to her body when he gave her one of those looks. Or when she heard that growl in his throat. Or when she stood too damn close to him behind the bar. Lori flicked the screen in one final act of desperation.

"Accessibility mode off," it finally called out, sounding disappointed.

Lori sighed. She'd turned it off, but the damage was already done. That was exactly what she deserved for thinking it was a good idea to wear that damn thing in there and have it count whatever steps she took while working.

"Lori."

She turned on her heel. Rex was right behind her. Those eyes were ablaze now, burning deep into her soul and waking her up all over again. She didn't need to look at her wrist to see that her heartbeat was up because she could feel her blood coursing through every part of her body. She swallowed, knowing that he knew. He had to, and she was about to get fired. Even though the customers liked her and she made good drinks, now was the moment he'd decide that she just couldn't stay. She braced herself, waiting for it.

Instead, he grabbed her by the waist and pressed his mouth against hers, his stubble brushing against her skin as his tongue teased her lips open. Lori moaned, surprised and thrilled by this change of plans. A shiver of pleasure whipped through her body as he leaned her back onto the table she'd just cleaned. The two chairs that'd already been put up on the other side of it clattered to the floor, bouncing as they hit the wood. Rex didn't seem to care as he pressed his body closer to hers.

Lori let the rag she held fall to the floor as she wrapped her arms around his broad back. God, he felt even sexier than he looked. He was so big and burly, making her feel tiny and delicate in his rough embrace. She traced her fingers over the muscles of his back, enjoying the hard plains under her hands. Her touch extended upward to find that even the back of his neck was hard before she stroked her fingertips through his hair. The short buzz on either side of his scalp sent another frisson of energy through her, and she buried her fingers in the longer locks on top.

The velvety feel of his tongue against hers made Lori want the kiss to continue through the night, but she dropped her head to the table's surface as he left her mouth and traced his tongue down the side of her neck.

"I've wanted you since the day I first saw you," he growled against her throat, his teeth raking across the surface of her skin.

She didn't answer. She didn't know *how* to answer. Had any man ever talked to her like that? It was the sort of seduction that every woman dreamed of when reality was usually a quick bit of cardio to get the job done. As Rex had pushed her down onto the table, he'd straddled her legs around him. She could feel his hardness throbbing against her, and she only managed a small whimper in response.

His grip on her thighs tightened, pulling her hard against his body. His lips roved lower, grazing her collarbone. "Tell me. You feel it, too. Don't you."

It wasn't a question. How could she deny it? Rex had haunted her mind ever since she'd first opened her eyes and seen his handsome face staring down at her. She'd thought it was an odd coincidence that she'd see him again so soon and then even end up employed at his club, but Lori was starting to think it was so much more than that. "Yes," she breathed.

His muscles quivered. Rex's body above her felt raw and dangerous, and her breath hitched as his mouth drifted over to the other side of her neck. "Tell me, Lori. Tell me you want me. I won't touch you any further unless you do."

Her body ached with need for him. She could feel it in him, too. He was holding himself back, and that knowledge made a whole new rush of desire blaze through her. Lori stroked her hands down the side of his face and lifted his head, meeting his gaze. There was so much in those eyes. It was almost too much, but she wanted to see him. She wanted to see how he looked when he was waiting for her like that. It was more inti-mate than anything else they could do, and the feeling he gave her inside grew stronger. "I want you, Rex."

His capable hands quickly pulled her shirt up over her head, and his pupils nearly eclipsed his blue eyes as he freed her breasts from her bra. Lori gasped as the cool air of the club hit her nipples and made them stand at attention, but Rex quickly warmed them with his mouth.

Wanting to feel more of his skin against her, she reached around his back for the hem of his shirt.

He'd been hot enough even with his clothes on, but he was damn sexy now. His shoulders were wide and muscled, and just the right amount of dark curls covered his chest. They narrowed and trailed down his toned stomach into the waistband of his jeans, and she reached for the button.

He hardly gave her a chance as he tugged at her pants, and she felt the raking of his fingernails against her plump ass in his haste to get her cotton briefs off. Lori felt the hot heaviness of him against her. Even before he was inside, she felt her body tensing in all the right ways.

Planting his hands on either side of her, he looked deeply into her eyes as he slowly plunged inside. Lori gasped as he slid home, and a tremble of belonging burst within her. His next thrust was slow and deliberate, a test. The next one came harder and faster, her breathing sharp and quick as he pushed her against the surface of the table.

Did he have a clue what he was doing to her? Lori felt like she'd turned into another person, as though Rex had unlocked a new side of herself as she pulled him close. She felt him gliding inside her, that intense thrust at the end of the movement jolting her body. Her fingers curled, and when her nails raked down his back, his resulting growl was too satisfying. She felt *alive.*

Her muscles shivered as her body convulsed. Her hips arched toward him as the spasms racked her against the table and against him, her cries of rapture breaking free. Rex drove harder, faster, spurring her on into another convulsion. The table legs pounded against the floor as he drove into her. He wanted her, he had her, and now he was giving her more. Her nails dug in harder as she nipped the side of his neck, hardly able to stand this powerful sensation. Rex roared as he exploded, his voice joining hers.

Catching her breath, Lori looked around. The table they were on had danced across the floor and was up against another one. More chairs had fallen, but she hadn't even heard them. The remainder of the club slowly became evident around her, with Rex at the center.

He looked down at her with one eyebrow raised. "That's one hell of a way to put me in a better mood."

9

REX WOKE THE NEXT MORNING AS THE SUN ROSE. HE rolled over and shoved his face into the pillow, desperate to go back to sleep. It was far too early for someone who worked the shift he did to be awake.

Besides, he'd been dreaming about Lori. The perfume of her skin still haunted him, something sweet and earthy that drove his wolf wild. The way her hair had splayed out on that table made him want to revisit the scene and time just to trace his eyes over those gentle waves. Her body had felt exquisite beneath him, and she'd drawn him into her as though he belonged there.

Damn it.

Rex flung the thin blanket off and stormed into his adjoining bathroom. He shouldn't be thinking about her like that for a number of reasons. For one, Lori was his employee. Sure, he owned the business, and he could do whatever the hell he wanted, but Rex knew that even he was more responsible than that.

Then there was the fact they'd done it right there in the bar. Granted, that'd been the hottest sex of his life. The two of them had been circling each other ever since she'd come to work at Selene's. It only seemed appropriate that their lust for each other should be acted upon there, no matter how inappropriate it was. And hell, the way she'd looked in his eyes and told him she wanted him? Rex had to muster unbelievable strength to keep his wolf under control.

He shook his head, sending water flying out of his hair to splat against the shower curtain liner. There he went again, thinking about their little tryst like it was something romantic, something exciting, something that would ever happen again.

Pulling down the shower head to rinse the suds down the drain, Rex knew there was only one reason this was a problem. No one would care that he'd had sex with an employee. They probably wouldn't even care that it'd happened at the club, mostly because they would never know about it.

It was the fact that Lori was human.

When he stepped out of the shower and some of the steam had cleared from the mirror, Rex took a moment to look at himself. He needed to remember just who he was. If some lower-level pack member fucked around with a human, it would probably just be for a good laugh or a power play. But him? He was the Alpha of the Glenwood pack. He was not only in charge, he was a role model for the rest of the pack. He couldn't have anything to do with a human beyond letting them be guests at his club, and even he had to admit that bringing Lori on the staff had been pushing it.

A red mark showed on his lower neck in the mirror. Rex stepped closer to examine it. He hadn't paid much attention to it last night. He'd come home and had fallen into bed, as he usually did. The hot water had made it redder and more swollen, and now he couldn't miss it. Lori must have nipped him a little harder than he'd thought.

It wasn't anything like a mate mark. It was tiny, left with feeble human teeth that weren't good for anything beyond chewing a good steak. But Rex remembered the flood of desire that coursed through his veins when she'd done that, and he'd never wanted anyone more. It'd been incredible. His wolf within had awakened even further, barely held back.

How could something so good be so wrong?

"Oh, Rex. There you are, dear. What's the matter?" Joan stopped in the middle of the hallway and tipped her head as she studied his face.

"Nothing." It wasn't true, but it was his standard answer, regardless. That meant it shouldn't be a surprise.

"Mmm. No." Joan shook her head of curly gray hair, and her crystal bracelets clacked softly as she reached up to touch his cheek. "You might fool everyone else but not me. There's something very different about you this morning."

Yes, but it wasn't anything he was going to discuss. Especially with his mother. "Everything's fine." He skirted past her and continued down the hallway.

"I got the Knight of Wands this morning," she called out behind him.

He turned to her, skeptical. "Didn't you tell me a long time ago that you're not supposed to pull tarot cards for someone unless they ask you to?"

"And didn't you tell me that I should do what needs to be done because I'm the oracle of this pack?" she challenged. Her back was straight and proud as she moved toward him. "You know what this card means, don't you?"

"No," he replied honestly. How in the world she memorized every single one of them was beyond him. He returned to his mission for breakfast and headed toward the kitchen. "I don't want to, either."

That wasn't enough to deter her. Joan followed him in, leaning on the counter as he opened the fridge and scanned its contents. "The Knight of Wands is a card of heated passion, one that manifests itself swiftly. It's telling you to have confidence because your true mate is closer than ever."

His guts cranked into a twisted knot, and he shut the fridge. Coffee sounded better than a meal, anyway. "You've been saying that sort of thing for a long time, Mom."

"No," she corrected quickly. "I said your mate would be someone special. I never gave you a timeline, but it looks like the cards are being more than just a little suggestive."

"I don't have time for this." He opened a cabinet door and fished out a mug.

Joan gave him a look. "You know, you can doubt it all you want, but the cards tell us what we need to know. You can't just deny the passion between two people, and the chemistry when they're mates is just divine! Why, your father and I—"

"That's enough of that," he interrupted. "I really don't need to hear the rest of that sentence."

She lifted a shoulder. "Suit yourself, but you're missing out on a good story. But I'm telling you, Rex. I'm so confident in this that I'd be willing to use any other technique you could name, and I'd get the same result." With a whirl of her tasseled scarf, she headed back down the hall.

Rex pinched the bridge of his nose and closed his eyes, but not because of the cloud of patchouli his mother had left behind her. She had no idea what havoc her prediction wrought on him. Was she trying to say that *Lori* was the person he'd been waiting for? Being human, he supposed, would make her special in a way, but it wasn't the sort of way that the rest of the pack would accept. Or was Joan simply trying to say that his *real* mate, the wolf he'd been fated to his whole life, was just around the corner? He needed clarification, but he didn't dare ask her for it. That would mean having to explain himself, and he sure as shit wasn't going to do that.

With a travel mug of coffee in his hand and far too many doubts in his mind, he headed to work.

He was the first one to arrive, as usual. Rex

glanced at the table where everything had happened as he flicked on the lights and unlocked the door. It was innocently back in its place, as were all the chairs. Rex had sent Lori home and told her he would finish cleaning up, so he'd known it would be just as it should've been when he walked in. Still, that particular table felt different to him now. His wolf stirred within as he recognized the lingering scent of their wild tryst the night before.

Stepping behind the bar, he entered his office and left the door open. He rubbed his hands over his face while the computer booted up. This was his routine, and it was exactly what he needed. He would go through the same motions he always did, eventually making him feel like he was normal again.

He started his routine by checking the day's schedule. The first thing Rex noticed was that Lori wasn't on it. He curled his fist in frustration. Was there not a damn thing he could do without thinking about her?

It was safer to move on to his next task, which was to see what bands would be playing that night. Rex frowned as he thought about the band that'd canceled, and he hoped it wouldn't happen again. Was there any chance that Lori's presence was actually chasing people away from his club? Would Dave's prediction come true, and all of the best shifter bands would find other places to play just because he had a human on staff?

But that was another thought about Lori. So much for distracting himself with his routine.

The outer door opened and shut. "Damn. Is anyone else picking up on that?"

"Picking up on what?" Rex replied from his office. He could tell by the voice alone that it was Randy.

"Someone totally fucked in here last night." Randy stepped into the office and immediately made a face. "Did you see any groupies hanging out with the band last night?"

Rex smirked, knowing he'd been caught. "It wasn't a groupie."

Randy stared at him, his eyes widening. "You've gotta be kidding me."

Randy did okay with the rougher crowd because he had no manners and genuinely gave zero fucks about what anyone thought of him. He was an over-grown punk who was more than happy to bring beers and shots to the guests if it meant he got to sneak in a few himself. "Nope. But I cleaned the whole place last night, so quit your bitching and get to work."

"It smells like... I don't know... like..."

"Human." Dave stepped in behind him, filling the doorway.

"Dude," Randy said, "you hooked up with a human here?"

"Not just any human. Lori," Dave said, his dark eyes narrowing. "I can't believe you let her leave a mark on you."

"What?" Randy asked, far too loudly for the small space. He leaned over to get a look at the curve between Rex's shoulder and neck. "Holy shit. Is that what that is?"

"You let the others bring her to our packhouse and risked her knowing who we are. Then you bring her into this club, keeping her right here among us. Now this?" Dave's jaw flexed. "I didn't know an Alpha was capable of betraying his own pack that deeply."

"Fuck off." Rex slammed his hands onto the arm of the chair and launched himself to his feet, pushing past Dave and Randy. It was too tight in there with them breathing down his neck, not to mention staring at it. Even the long strip of space behind the bar wasn't enough, and he moved out onto the open area used as a dance floor. He grabbed the broom, needing something to do to diffuse all the tension building inside him.

"How can you denigrate yourself like that and expect the rest of us to still have a shred of respect for you?" Dave growled. He'd come out and now stood just in front of the bar, his chest puffed and his fists curled.

"Yeah!" Randy chimed in.

Rex turned around, letting the broom clatter to the floor, and strode over to Dave. "It's your duty to be on the lookout for threats, but you should be smart enough to know that they aren't coming from me, or Lori, for that matter."

"Ugh!" Dave arched his head back. "I can't even speak to you with that pathetic mark on your neck! If you've got some sick fetish, maybe the pack would be better off in different hands."

Without thinking, Rex shoved Dave backward, who landed hard against the front of the bar. Rex stepped up to him, giving him no room to leave. Randy hovered on the side, but Rex wasn't worried about him. His dark blue eyes had turned silver, and he kept his gaze locked on Dave's. "I could choose to see that as a threat, you know. It's a threat you'd be very stupid to make. I'm sick of everyone telling me what to do, especially when it has nothing to do with them. I'm the one in charge. If you don't like my personal life, leave."

The corner of Dave's eye twitched. He was trying to control himself; Rex could feel it. Dave's wolf was writhing inside of him, ready to come out and fight. Rex almost wished he'd try so he'd have the excuse to give him the hell he deserved.

They could stand there like that all day, but Rex was ready for this bullshit to be over with. "Go home for the day. Both of you. Without pay."

"Hey!" Randy protested. "I'm already behind on rent."

"Maybe you should've thought of that before you opened your mouth and challenged your Alpha," Rex reminded him. "Now get the fuck out of here. I'll run the place myself today. It'll be easier than dealing with you."

The door slammed behind them, and Rex picked up the broom.

"By yourself?" a voice said from the far corner of the club. "I don't count?"

"Max." Rex turned to face his brother. "I didn't hear you come in."

"You were busy," Max said, as though that fully encompassed everything that'd happened between

Rex and the other two. "I thought it was best to hang back, just in case you needed me."

It wasn't the wrong thing to do, but Rex hated that Max even thought he had to. "I was fine."

"It seems so." Max started taking the chairs down off the tables.

"Go on home," Rex said quietly.

"I can handle—"

"It's not a matter of whether or not you can handle it." Rex sliced his hand through the air to cut off any further thoughts of that. "I just want to be alone, and I want to work."

"You're going to be exhausted by the end of the night if you do that to yourself." Max pulled another chair down.

"That's the point. Just go on. I'm fine."

His beta paused, looking at him for a long moment before he finally turned to go.

Rex sighed, and the sound echoed in the empty space. Before long, a band would take the stage. The tables would be full, and so would the dance floor. He'd hardly be able to keep up with the drink orders. Hell, he'd probably piss a few of his customers off. Well, good. That was fine with him as long as it meant he didn't have to think about Lori or all the trouble she'd caused.

No. He couldn't blame her. Surely, Lori had never asked to accidentally catch a wolf pack shifting before a run. She'd come into his club looking for a job, but she had no idea who ran it. Had she intended to shake up his life so much, he hardly recognized himself? Rex had no idea.

He said a silent prayer to Selene, begging for guidance.

10

LORI FROWNED AT THE PHONE WHEN SHE HEARD IT ring. Of course someone had to call her right now while she was in the middle of getting ready for work and needed to get out the door in five minutes. Would anyone have bothered to call when she was doing nothing but puttering around her apartment, trying to decide where to put things? Of course not.

Then she saw it was Conner, and some of her anger melted away. "Hi, honey."

"Hey, Mom. What's wrong?"

"Hm? Nothing's wrong." She put the phone on speaker and set it down on the bathroom counter so she could finish doing her makeup. "Why?"

"I don't know. You sound tired or sick or something."

She frowned at the phone again, but this time for a different reason. It was nice to think that Conner would pay enough attention to know if she wasn't feeling well, but it also felt like an insult if he thought she sounded that way. "I'm fine. I'm a little crabby, that's all."

"Okay, if you're sure. Coach said some viruses are going around right now, and he's all freaked out about it because he doesn't want to be short any players."

"Are *you* feeling all right?" she asked, wondering if this was his way of saying he was the one who was sick. His father had been weird about illness. Chuck would never admit he was sick, claiming he was far too strong for the germs to bother him. Then, when he'd finally gotten so bad that he had to admit defeat, he'd curl up in bed and demand to be taken care of like a child. Conner was more mature than that, she knew, but she hadn't figured out just how much of Chuck was in him.

"I'm fine," he insisted. "I just wondered if you wanted to get together again next week for dinner."

Her reflection developed a deeper wrinkle between her eyebrows. Like she had time to cook again! She was busy enough, and—

"You know, there *is* something wrong with me."

She put down her mascara and straightened, trying to analyze herself.

"What? What is it?"

"It's nothing bad, so don't freak out on me. It's just perimenopause."

The phone was silent for a long moment. "Huh?"

"It means I'm getting older," she explained, wondering what they taught kids in sex ed classes, anyway. There was much more to life than wearing deodorant and using condoms. "I'm having horrible hot flashes, especially at night or when I get out of the shower. I'm so hot inside sometimes that I just want to stick my head in the freezer. My mood swings have been pretty terrible, too. One minute I'm excited about organizing my new apartment, and the next, I'm pissed off about having to do it at all."

"Oh. Okay. Well, that sucks."

She smiled, knowing the poor kid had no idea what to say. "That's not even the half of it. I've been having very strange nightmares, probably from the hormone swings. My periods have been getting all weird and—"

"Mom! I don't want to know about old lady stuff like that!"

She stifled a laugh, as well as the urge to bring up breast tenderness. Lori had traumatized him enough. She picked up her curling iron to touch up her waves. "Fair enough. It does suck right now, but I'll be okay. You'll just have to put up with me being cranky for a while."

Conner laughed a little at that. "Whatever you say, Mom. So, do you still want to do dinner again?"

There was no mood swing that could truly keep her from wanting to say yes to that. He was the whole reason she'd moved to Eugene, and the fact that he'd called her to ask about it meant the world to her. "Sure, honey. Let me just check my work schedule and see what day is best."

"Okay."

"And I'm not old," she added.

He laughed again. "Okay, Mom! Bye!"

When she'd hung up, she looked in the mirror. Perimenopause definitely meant she was getting older, but it didn't have to mean she was ancient. She turned her face one way and then the other. Lori didn't look the same way she had in high school, and she'd noticed fine lines that hadn't been there before, but she was satisfied enough. Smiling, she thought Rex must be as well.

She felt far too hot for a January day, and her lack of sleep was evident in the heaviness of her eyelids, but Lori put on her boots and headed out the door anyway. She needed this job no matter how shitty she felt, and it wouldn't be the first time she'd stood on her feet all night when she ought to be in bed. Lori had been both the owner of a saloon and a mother, so she certainly knew what it was like to push through.

"Hey," she said as she came in through the back door of Selene's, finding Rex standing behind the bar.

He was leaning forward with his elbows resting on the wood, reading through a stack of papers in front of him. "Hey."

She hung up her coat. It was going to be hard enough to figure out how to handle whatever this was between them without worrying about remaining conscious throughout her shift.

Lori clocked in. Rex had given her the most toe-curling, mind-blowing night of her life. It was so damn good that she'd wanted to call Abbie about it immediately, even though it was the middle of the night, but it was also so good that she didn't want to spoil it by telling anyone.

She took a glance at the schedule and saw that, once again, she was slated to work only with him, although she'd sworn some of the others had been listed before. Was that on purpose? Had something changed, and if so, what did that mean? Had Dave said something to Rex and now refused to work with her? Well, if he did, she wouldn't lose sleep over it. That asshole could keep his distance.

"How's the stock in the fridge?" she asked.

"Already took care of it."

Hm. Was he being distant or just his usual gruff self? It wasn't like he ever stood around making small talk while they opened the club. Lori went into the stock room to get a package of napkins. She popped open the paper seal around them and brought them back into the front to load them into the dispenser so they'd be ready for use. She was thinking about this too much. Just because they had sex didn't mean it was some romantic thing. Sure, her body was telling her just how much she'd like to have more encounters with him, even though she felt like hell. But that didn't mean it was anything more than a physical connection. Wasn't that what people did these days? They hooked up and then acted like it didn't matter?

Chucking the paper wrapper into the recycling bin, she saw that the straws were low and went back into the storeroom. Lori knew she should've grabbed both things at once to be more efficient, but her mind didn't want to let that happen. She felt like she was in a fog, or maybe still in that dream she'd had last night.

She leaned against the shelf and closed her eyes as she tried to remember it. She was outside, under the moon. The earth was cold under her feet, but it felt good. She was looking for something, but she couldn't find it. That yearning still existed inside her, even in the waking world, but Lori no longer had any idea just what she was looking for. She shrugged and realized she shouldn't focus on a dream so hard. All that really mattered was getting her work done and then going home. She could crash like she wanted to, and maybe tomorrow, she could look up some supplements that would help.

Bringing the package of straws out to the bar, it took all of her concentration just to take a handful out of the box and place them in the little rack where they kept them for easy access.

"Are you okay?"

Lori looked up to see Rex standing beside her, his eyes scrutinizing.

"Um…" How could she tell him? It wasn't as though she were sick, and this would just go away if she went home and slept it off. Perimenopause could last for a long time, with some days being better than others. It was real, but she couldn't tell him about it. *Oh, I'm fine. It's just that the woman you banged is having hot flashes and temper tantrums.* Right. That's what she wanted to do. "I'm just a little tired today."

He stared at her for another moment before he nodded. "Okay."

Her shoulders relaxed as he moved off to the other side of the club. Lori reminded herself that she needed to do a better job of faking it. If he wasn't convinced, he'd send her home. Then she wouldn't get paid, and that would send her in the absolute opposite direction she was trying to go. Having steady income was a huge relief, but she was still making up for the big deposit she'd had to put down for the apartment.

The first band came in and started to set up, which at least meant that Rex was distracted. Lori let him go talk to them about sound and lights while she took care of the first customers, the ones who didn't mind if the band was playing just yet.

"Just need a beer," the first guy said.

Good. Easy. All she had to do was pull the draught and hand it over. She could do that if she were sleepwalking. If she took everything just one step at a time, she'd be fine.

But the crowd continued to pick up, and the

more people came in the door, the more panicked she started to feel. They were all coming at her at once, all demanding one thing or another. She sucked in a breath, trying to force air into her lungs. Something felt so strange inside her. It was similar to the feeling Rex gave her when he stood too close or accidentally brushed her arm. It was in the same place inside of her, but this time, it wasn't pleasant. She was angry that so many people were coming into the club, as though it were her home and it was being invaded.

"I'm going fucking crazy," she muttered to herself as she mixed a quick Bloody Mary. This was more than just something she could take a supplement for. She'd have to find a new doctor there in Eugene and hope they didn't send her to a mental institution.

The band was banging away, but it wasn't music. It was loud and raucous noise just for the sake of noise, and it only made her angrier. As that continued to foam and froth inside of her, Lori's body continued to betray her. Her stomach churned. She bumped her hip on the corner of the bar and tripped over a table leg as though she had no idea what the parameters of her own body were again. But she gritted her teeth and forced herself to go on.

If she was already there, she'd be damned if she wasn't going to finish her shift.

When the last band was on, she'd reached her limit. One of the dreaded hot flashes reared its ugly head. She felt the flames expanding within, singeing the underside of her skin. Even her breath felt hot, and she couldn't escape the burning sensation. Lori leaned against the bar and flapped her hand in front of her face, trying to cool off. She longed to go outside and just lay on the cold sidewalk, something she'd done a few times when she'd been pregnant with Conner and had experienced hot flashes. That couldn't happen now, and that knowledge only made the panic set in more.

Suddenly, like a blessing out of nowhere, something cold pressed against the back of her neck. Lori's shoulders relaxed. She leaned her elbows on the bar and put her face in her hands. "Thank you," she whispered.

The cold can of beer rotated slightly. "You're welcome. You're not really okay, are you?"

"I thought I was," she replied honestly. "Now I'm not so sure. I thought it was just a hot flash, but..." Lori hadn't meant to tell him about that initially, but it was obvious that he could tell. At least he didn't seem to mind.

"Come here." Rex took her by the elbow and brought her into his office. He gently led her down into his desk chair and handed her the can of beer while he pulled over the other chair and picked up her legs to put her feet in the seat. Rex disappeared for a moment, but he returned and draped a cold, wet rag over her head. He turned off the overhead light, leaving only a small lamp on in the corner. "What's going on?"

Lori looked up at him numbly. Those small gestures had made the worst of it go away, even if she didn't exactly feel like jumping to her feet. His eyes were still hard, but she thought it was more with concern than agitation. "I really don't know, Rex. I haven't been feeling well all day. I think it might just be hormonal stuff."

"Mm." His mouth twisted at the corner. Lori was prepared for him to get just as grossed out as Conner did. He shook his head. "I'm not a woman, but I think it's something else. You shouldn't be here, but I don't think you should drive home, either. You stay here and relax, and as soon as I can close down for the night, I'll take you home."

Lori opened her mouth to protest that she could drive herself home or even that she could call her son, but he was already out of the office and shutting the door behind him softly. He was right, though. She didn't need to do anything right now but sit there in the semi-darkness for a bit, and she needed to be content with that.

Leaning back and closing her eyes, she saw Rex's face. He was always there in her mind. He was her boss. He was only taking care of her like this because of liability issues. He didn't want to get sued if he let her drive home and she got into a wreck or something. It didn't mean any more than that, just like their encounter the night before didn't go beyond two people satisfying a physical need.

If that were true, would he have helped her as he did when she'd fallen at the park? But they'd hardly known each other then, so it wasn't like he could've had feelings for her. And that wasn't to say he had any feelings now because Lori knew for sure that he didn't. Did he?

She flipped the rag to the cold side and sighed. If whatever was going on with her affected her brain this much, she was sicker than she thought.

11

SELENE'S WAS HOPPING. THE SHE-WOLVES WERE onstage, and always popular with Rex's regular crowd. He usually enjoyed their music himself, but he hardly heard a single note that night. All he could think about was Lori.

As he brought a tray of drinks to a table, he wondered what the hell was going on with her. His wolf strained toward her even though his work forced him to stay away. He wanted to make sure she was okay. More than that, he wanted to be able to fix whatever was wrong.

"Hey, can I get a shot of Jameson?" The regular standing at the bar had a huge, pointed stud that stuck out from his bottom lip. Even though he had quite a few other facial piercings, that one always stood out the most. The guy liked to pull his lips inward so the stud flexed in the air.

Rex had never asked his name. There were too many people to keep track of, and as long as they felt like he recognized them, they seemed happy enough. "Last one."

"You're cutting me off already?" Stud Lip protested.

"Gotta call it like I see it," Rex pointed out. Not only that, he wanted to get out of there as quickly as possible without having to wait for this guy.

Hell, he really must be hung up on Lori if he was ready to pull the plug on The She-Wolves and send everyone home.

Sliding that last shot of whiskey down the bar, Rex forced himself to stay on task. He checked on tables, took payments, and swept up the glass someone had dropped on the floor. Could he possibly be one of those shifters who fell for a human? Rex knew that it happened, but not in his pack. In fact, Rex was fairly sure there wasn't a drop of human blood in his whole family line. He'd ask his parents, but then they'd start asking him questions of their own.

The band finished their encore, and Rex flicked the lights on while they broke down their equipment. He waited impatiently for the crowd to shuffle out, cleaning up behind them and hoping they'd move along. They got the hint, but they didn't appreciate it. Rex felt a flash of irritation as he imagined one of them complaining to Dave the next time they saw him, which would only give Dave more ammo.

When the band had hauled out the last of their equipment and the crowd had left, Rex locked up. He slowly opened the door to the office and found Lori in the same position he'd left her in. Even lying back, sick as a dog, he could see the beauty in her face. He almost hated to disturb her, but she sat up and took the rag off her forehead.

"I'm really sorry. How long have I been in here?"

"A bit." He hadn't exactly kept track of time. "I'm going to take you home now. And don't apologize."

"Why not?" she asked as she slowly put her feet on the floor and rubbed her hand over the side of her face. "I left you to run the club on your own."

Something he'd willingly done just the day before. "It's not the first time, and it won't be the last. Are you feeling any better?"

"Mostly. I don't know what's going on with me today. My body feels like crap, but so does my mind. I just don't really feel like myself."

He wasn't a doctor, and he was already doing

what little he was capable of to help. "Maybe you just need a good night's rest."

She allowed him to help her to her feet. "I guess."

Rex noticed how slowly she was moving, and his worry grew. When he helped her into her jacket, he felt the burning heat of her skin. "Are you still having hot flashes?"

"No." She looked up at him with clearer eyes than she'd had before. "I'm just tired now."

"Right." He was overthinking every detail, a bad habit he'd formed ever since Lori had come into his life.

"Oh, you didn't clean up the merch area," Lori noted as they passed by. "I'll come in early tomorrow morning and help you."

"No," he insisted quickly. He was fully aware that most of their closing routine hadn't been performed, but he didn't care. It would be fine, and he didn't want her to worry about it. "I've got it."

She tried to give him a stubborn look, but it was a watered-down version of the one he was used to.

The night was cold around them as they headed out the back door. Rex wished he'd started his truck earlier so it'd already be warmed up by the time they got in. She stumbled, leaning into him to regain her balance. Automatically, Rex put his arm around her, that warm floral scent of her perfume flooding his senses.

"Well, well, well." Dave stepped out from the shadows. His hands were loosely in his pockets, and his head was tipped back so he looked down at Rex, regardless of their similar heights. "I guess neither of you wanted to take my warnings seriously."

Immediately, Rex's wolf was on guard. Warnings? What had he said to Lori? "Fuck off, Dave. I'm trying to get her home."

"Yeah." Dave looked down at Lori with a wicked smile on his face. "That's not going to happen. She's coming with me."

He could feel Lori stiffen under his arm. "It's all right."

"No," Dave said with a little laugh. "It's really not." Two more shadows stepped out from behind him.

Rex fully expected Randy to be there, as well as Adam. The two of them were thick as thieves with Dave. "I'm giving you one last chance to get the hell out of here."

Dave's dark eyes lifted to Rex's. His pupils changed before anything else, narrowing and leaving behind bright golden irises that nearly shone in the darkness. Dave flicked his head back as his fangs emerged. He lunged through the air, his hands and feet changing into paws on the fly as he hurtled toward Lori.

Rex heard her scream, and the sound twisted his heart as his own wolf exploded through his skin. This wasn't the way for anyone to find out. He'd been trying to avoid it ever since he'd first laid eyes on her, but there was no helping it now. She knew his secret, and nothing would be the same again.

Rex clashed with Dave before he could get to Lori. The two wolves tumbled to the ground, a tangle of fur and paws. Dave's white teeth flashed as he sought to get a grip on Rex's throat, but Rex managed to dodge to the right just as they snapped shut.

What the fuck do you think you're doing? he asked through his pack's mental link. Jumping to his feet, Rex took a wide stance and bared his teeth to remind Dave who was in charge.

"Rex?" Lori called weakly.

In his peripheral vision, he could see her slumped down against the back of the building. Randy and Adam had shifted as well, now circling her as if she were their prey.

What's the matter? Dave taunted as he moved to

join them. *Aren't you gonna go save your pathetic human? Or are you finally going to fight me like a true Alpha?*

Rex growled, beyond furious. *You think I don't have control of this pack? You're the one who's out of control!*

Actually, I'm the one who's going to be in control once I'm done here. Dave aligned himself so that he and his goons stood between Rex and Lori. *And that means I'll decide what happens to her.*

Rex held strong, ready for the attack that he knew would come. They were just trying to keep him distracted with talk about Lori. *This isn't about her. It's about you and me. Leave her out of this.*

Not a fucking chance.

With one small flick of Dave's head, he, Randy, and Adam pounced toward Rex. The Alpha braced for the impact, skidding along the asphalt. Claws dug into his flank, and he felt the trickle of blood soak his fur. Teeth snapped near his ears, and Rex ducked his head. They were on top of him now, heavy and determined. He was outnumbered. They could do whatever they wanted to him, but Lori was a different story. Rage boiled up inside of him. Rex didn't want to hurt his packmates. His job was to protect them, but they hadn't given him a choice.

He lashed out blindly against the assault, his jaws snapping around a leg. Rex clamped down hard and yanked. The resulting pop echoed in his bones, but the howl of pain that issued from Randy told him he'd done his job. The pale wolf pulled back immediately, desperately yanking his injured leg out of Rex's mouth.

Adam hadn't given up. His snarls grew ferocious as he tried to pin Rex with his paws. Saliva dripped from his fangs as he dug his teeth down through the thick fur of Rex's ruff.

Rex could sense how confident Adam was and used it to his advantage. It was almost painful to do so, but Rex went limp. Adam's head popped back, and he turned to look at Dave. *The scared bastard gave up!*

That was all the room that Rex needed. He flipped to his paws and pushed himself up before Adam could react. The other wolf's neck was out of his grasp, so he latched onto the only thing available and snapped his teeth around Adam's muzzle. His sharp fangs easily pierced the sensitive skin around Adam's nose, and blood filled his mouth.

The yelp that issued from his throat echoed against the back of the building. Adam's claws scratched against the ground as he fought to get

away from Rex, pulling backward. When Rex finally
let go, the other wolf went flying.

Get your asses back in there and finish the job! Even
in his head, Dave's voice was loud and angry.

Fuck this, Randy said, limping away from the
scene.

I'm with you. Adam joined him, and they scam-
pered off into the shadows toward the woods.

"Rex?" Lori was breathing heavily now, and her
head lolled to the side. "Is that really you? Am I
hallucinating?"

Rex hated himself for it, but there was nothing
he could do for her right now. He couldn't even tell
her that things would be okay, not only because he
wasn't in human form but also because he wasn't
entirely sure they would be. He could only listen to
her whimpering and tried to tune it out. He faced
Dave, his hackles up and his paws spread to keep
him balanced. *This is what you wanted anyway. If you
wanted to challenge me so badly, then all you had to do
was say so.*

His enemy moved slightly away from Lori to get
out onto even ground where he could attack more
fully. *Fine. Just you and me.*

Rex pulled in a deep breath. Steam rose from his
nostrils. He'd be damned if he attacked first and let

Dave have an excuse to return to the pack with a bad word to say about him. Rex was already bleeding from his flank and his haunches where Adam had trampled him. It would heal quickly enough once he could change back, but he had to make it through the rest of this fight first. He spared a thought for the pack, for what could happen to them if he couldn't defeat Dave.

Rex!

The distinctly female voice filled his mind. He shouldn't have, but Rex swung his head to the side.

Where Lori had been a moment ago now stood a wolf. Her brilliant white fur blazed under the moonlight, her violet eyes uncertain but enchanting as she watched the men.

Lori?

Dave growled deeply. *You didn't tell me your bitch was a she-wolf.*

That was because he hadn't known. Rex felt that same tug he always had toward her, and he understood. It all made so much sense now, yet at the same time, it didn't make sense at all. Adrenaline bolted through his veins as he tried to figure out how to handle this.

There wasn't time. Dave charged at him, aiming first for the wounds near his hind leg. He sliced one of the lacerations further open, sending a burning pain through Rex's muscles. It gave Rex an opening to Dave's soft underbelly. He bit hard and pulled away, sending a warm gush of blood to the ground.

A flash of white moved through his vision. Rex lurched to his feet to find that Lori had joined them. She had dashed around to Dave's other side, trying to distract him from fighting Rex. She snarled as she glared at Dave.

Get back, Lori. I've got this. His heart pounded loudly in his ears, terrified of what Dave might do to her if he had the chance.

She didn't respond, nor did she go away. Her thick tail swished through the air, and her ears swiveled one way and then the other. A growl emanated from her chest.

Oh, that's cute. I guess I get to take her out in wolf form. It's not what I expected, but I'll take it.

Dave hurled toward her, his teeth gnashing.

Rex could feel the fear in her, but she stood her ground. He flung himself after Dave, ignoring the burning pain in his side and the blood dripping down his leg. Summoning all his strength, Rex sprang into the air, landing to the side of Dave's spine and throwing him down to the ground. His jaw opened wide, and he buried his fangs in the fur of his opponent's neck, letting the sharp tips just pierce the thick hide underneath before he paused.

Well? Dave prompted. *Finish me already. That's what you've always wanted to do, anyway.*

It wasn't, but Rex wouldn't bother correcting him. *I could kill you right now with one snap of my jaw. Instead, I command you to retreat. You, Randy, and Adam are forever banished from the pack, just as Silas was for his antics with the Thompson bears up in Carlton. Never show your faces among us again.* His breath was heavy in his lungs as he waited for Dave's answer.

Fine. When Rex stepped back, Dave got to his feet. He glared at Lori one last time before bolting off in the same direction that Randy and Adam had gone.

12

Fear and confusion invaded her mind, but pain invaded her body. Lori felt her bones twisting and cracking. Her insides moved in startling ways, adjusting and shifting to make room. A dull fog descended over her vision and hearing, but once she stood on two feet again, she realized it was only the feeling of being human again. She stared down at her hands, which had been snow-white paws only a moment ago. "What the fuck just happened?"

Rex—or the beast she assumed to be Rex—was watching her with curiosity. With a flick of his head, his muzzle melted into a human face and his fur receded. He rolled his shoulders as if they were stiff, but not with the blistering pain that had seared through her own body and still lingered. "You tell me," he said, very much a human again.

She gaped up at him. "Me? You're the one who did it first!"

He flung his hands in the air and let them fall to his sides as he paced a slow circle. "I don't know whether to be pissed off or proud. Why didn't you tell me? You could've saved me a hell of a lot of trouble. Both of us, actually."

"And you don't think you could've told me?" she returned, pressing her hands against her legs to make sure they were real. "I didn't know anything about this, but you sure seemed to know what you were doing!"

"Wait." He stopped pacing and stared at her. Walking up slowly, he crouched down in front of her. "Are you saying you've never shifted before?"

"Um, *yeah*. That's exactly what I'm saying. I'm still not entirely sure this isn't some perimenopause fever dream, although I don't remember my doctor telling me hallucinations would be a symptom." Her stomach turned, but Lori didn't think it had anything to do with hormones. The wolf she'd just been, was that the thing inside her that'd been trying to get out all this time? Was that the feeling she couldn't quite identify or make sense of?

He cursed under his breath. "It wasn't a hallu-cination."

Lori swallowed. "Really? You're telling me that I actually turned into a wolf? And that you did, too?"

"Yes, as well as the others." He ran a hand through his hair and looked at the ground.

"I don't understand." She shook her head. Was she going to wake up from this nightmare anytime soon? "This can't be real. Maybe a customer slipped us some mushrooms tonight for a laugh. You never know what kind of stuff those headbangers might be carrying around."

"No." His voice was curt and authoritative. "Lori, I'm telling you, this doesn't have anything to do with drugs. There are shifters in the world who can turn into another creature at will. Some of them are bears or lions, or in our case, wolves. There are quite a few of us, actually."

It felt much more real to hear him say it. "Why didn't you tell me before?"

He let out a short bark of a laugh. "For one thing, I thought you were human, and shifters don't go around telling their secret to humans. It's not exactly safe."

She opened her mouth to protest, but then closed it again. She could see why it was a rather sensitive subject. She didn't even know if she'd tell anyone. "Life has been so weird ever since I came to Eugene."

"Weirder than you even know." Rex stood. He reached down to take her hand and help her to her feet. "You remember that day you woke up at my house?"

"Sure." She'd thought about it a million times, but now her nerves all came to attention as she waited to hear what he had to say about it.

His body was so close that she could feel his heat, even with the chill of the night air around them. "You went for a jog in the park, but you wandered pretty far off the main trail. You already know that. But then you stumbled upon some of the others shifting while you were out there. You saw them, and you ran off. That's when you tripped and hit your head."

She touched the place near her temple where the knot had been. "And that's why I don't remember the part about the wolves?"

His lips tightened. "Actually, no. My sister is not only a wolf shifter but a great healer, a talent she got from our mother's side of the family. I asked her to erase your memory of that. I couldn't risk having you tell other people what you saw."

"Ho-ly hell." She stepped back, realizing that Rex wasn't who she thought he was. Not at all. "That's... that's not right, Rex! You can't just go around erasing people's memories!"

"Hey." He put his hands on her arms, making her realize she'd been flapping them angrily. "It's not something I wanted to do, but just think for a second about what would've happened to you if you'd told someone. They'd think you were nuts. I did you a favor."

She huffed a breath out through her nose. "I highly doubt that was your motive."

"I felt guilty about it, okay?" He still had his hands on her arms and curled his fingers around the sleeves of her jacket. "It's a secret I've had to keep from you, along with my identity. *Our* identity, apparently. I didn't exactly enjoy it."

Something bubbled up inside of Lori. She didn't expect it to be laughter, so she was surprised when a chuckle escaped her throat. The irony made her snicker a little harder until she stood there sounding like an idiot laughing her ass off.

"What the hell is so funny?"

"All of this!" she exclaimed. "It's absolutely fucking ridiculous! I mean, I just turned into a goddamn wolf! That doesn't happen in real life. And even though I felt like absolute shit before this, somehow, I'm fine now. A little disturbed, but fine. It's like, was the creature just waiting to come out of me? And now that it has, everything's right as friggin' rain?"

Lori could hear the hysteria in her own voice, but she didn't care. This wasn't exactly easy to wrap her brain around. She laughed again, but that laughter slowly died as she realized just how tired she was. "I need to go home and go to bed."

"I think you need to come with me, actually." He looped his hand around her arm and began to lead her toward his truck.

"I can drive now, so it's all good," she insisted.

"No, Lori." He stopped and turned back to her, his face so close to hers, she thought he might kiss her. "There's a lot more I need to explain to you."

"But I'm exhausted." She truly was and didn't know if her brain could handle anything else. Could there really be more?

"I know." His voice was low and sympathetic. "But there's a lot you need to understand. You really shouldn't just go home and be alone. Not after that."

Lori twisted her lips, trying to decide. She thought about heading back to her place, where she'd left all the lights off and no one was waiting for her. Who would she talk to? What would happen if this... *thing* happened to her again? "I guess so."

"Good." He brought her around to the passenger side of his truck and helped her in. "I'll take you to the packhouse."

"Wait." Fear stiffened her muscles as he climbed behind the wheel. "Packhouse?"

"Like I said, there's a lot to explain." Rex fired up the engine and tapped the button to turn off the radio. "Many shifters live in groups, and of course, that would be a pack for wolves. It's a way to stay safe and have others around us who understand."

Her mouth dropped open as she understood the reality of what he was saying. "I don't think I want to do that, Rex. If there are other shifters there... I just... that's a lot."

"It's okay." His hand was warm when he laid it on her thigh. "You've already been there once."

She blinked. "I thought you said it was your place."

"It is. I'm the Alpha. I lead the whole pack, so essentially it is my place." He swung out onto the road.

Lori sank down in her seat. She'd felt perfectly fine once she'd become human again, but now her very human nerves were starting to take over. "This is crazy. Maybe you should just take me home. I can't handle this."

At the next stop sign, he turned to look at her. "You can still sense your wolf inside of you, can't you?"

She took a moment to analyze that. It was the most insane question anyone had ever asked her. Even the drunks she'd dealt with at both The Wagon Wheel and Selene's didn't say things as batshit as that. But what was even more absurd than his question was the fact she *did* feel it. Now that the wolf had come out once, she could sense it more strongly within her. Lori nodded.

"And what is it telling you?" he asked softly. "Does it want to run away from me? To go off and be alone? Or does it want to know more, to stay with someone you can trust?"

Lori didn't even know how to ask it, but it turned out she didn't need to. The animal inside her spoke to her without needing words or questions. The answers were simply there, a knowledge that she could feel. It wanted to be near him and didn't like the idea of being alone. "Fine. I'll come with you."

"Thank you." Someone had pulled up behind them at the stop sign, so Rex made his turn and continued on down the road.

Lori sat quietly. The world felt different around her. That feeling hadn't happened in a long time, and it sat oddly with her. She noticed that the tension between herself and Rex had melted away completely. Even the silence between them didn't feel strange. It turned out that he was right to tell her to stay with him because she realized she had an awful lot of questions.

"Why was Dave trying to kill us?" she asked as she watched a street sign slide by.

"Mostly because he's an asshole." Rex adjusted his grip on the steering wheel. "He was our pack's third in command. I allowed him to have that role because his father had held it before him, but clearly, he didn't deserve it, so I'll have to assign a new one soon. He was angry with me for hiring you because he thought it should be run strictly by shifters as it always had been before."

"Oh." Lori suddenly grasped just how many people she'd likely met who were shifters. It was a dizzying thought.

"He was also pretty irate when he found out we'd slept together," Rex added casually.

She sat up straighter again. "You told him?"

Rex shook his head. "I didn't have to. He picked up on the scent of it in the club."

"That's... weird." She turned beet red, not knowing what else to say. She clasped her hands together in her lap, wondering if this odd, tense feeling would ever go away. Why did it take forty-eight years to discover this other part of herself?

Rex made another turn, the reflection from the rearview mirror illuminating his eyes for a moment. "Now, I'd like to ask you a question."

She spread her fingers. "Have at it, but right now, I don't feel like I have a lot of answers."

"Did Dave confront you about working at Selene's? Back there, he'd said something about how neither one of us had heeded his warnings."

"Yeah." She'd nearly forgotten about that, considering everything else that'd happened. "He caught me out on the street one afternoon while I was taking a jog and made some vague threats, telling me I'd better quit my job. He scared the hell out of me, but I told him to kiss my ass."

A hint of a smile tilted the corner of Rex's mouth and then disappeared just as quickly as it'd come. "Why didn't you say anything to me about it?"

"I don't know," she admitted. "I was going to. Actually, I thought about calling the police first. Then I realized I didn't know enough about him to file a thorough report. So I figured I'd wait and talk to you about it, but then you were in a pissy mood, and I was questioning whether or not I should even take his threats seriously. I thought he might be one of those guys who thinks he can get people to do whatever he wants."

"Sounds about right."

Lori swallowed, thinking about the events that'd taken place right behind Selene's just a short time ago. It'd been terrifying to see Dave step out of the darkness like that. It'd been even more of a concern when he'd suddenly transformed into a wolf. Lori felt a little better knowing she had teeth of her own in a situation like that, but she still had to wonder about Dave. "Do you think he'll come back?"

"No," Rex answered immediately. "I banished him. He knows that if he or the others try to come back, they won't get off so easily the next time."

"Mmm." She understood, but she wasn't completely convinced.

"Listen, you're safe. Okay?" Rex pulled into a driveway, his headlights showing the cedar siding of a two-story house. The engine rumbled into silence, and Rex turned to her. "I know all of this is strange and new, but I promise everything will be okay from here on out."

The human side of her wasn't entirely sure.

People said things all the time, and even if they meant them, that didn't mean they could make them happen. But her wolf, so strong inside of her, felt otherwise. It'd already told her a few times that evening that Rex was someone to trust.

What choice did she have but to go along with it?

13

Rex got out of the truck and shut the door before walking around to Lori's side. He knew she was perfectly capable of getting out of the vehicle on her own, but seeing Dave go after her like that had activated every possessive and protective bone he had. He wanted to cover her with his own body and shield her from the world if that was what she needed. Rex bit his lip. He knew what those feelings meant, and if he were honest with himself, he'd known for a long time. That would be difficult to explain to Lori, but there would be time for that later.

Her hesitation was palpable as she stepped out and they walked through the garage. "I kind of wish I hadn't come."

"It's going to be fine." He would say it as many times as he needed to.

"It's just a lot." She paused just before they reached the interior door that led to the kitchen. "Rex, do you get to choose?"

"Choose what?" He felt his heartbeat thundering in his head, wondering if she was so attuned to him already that she understood what he'd been thinking about only a moment ago.

"Whether or not you're a wolf?" Her brown eyes implored him for all the answers she wanted.

Not what he'd been thinking, but that was fine. There was so much ground to cover. He would have to explain his entire lifestyle to her, and he couldn't exactly get it all out while standing there on the concrete steps, waiting to go into the house. He couldn't imagine what it had to be like for her, though. "You saw me earlier. I changed into my wolf and then back again at will."

"No." Her teeth played with her lip. "I mean, if I didn't want to be a shifter, would I get a choice? Is there something I did to make this happen to me?"

His soul buckled at the idea of Lori suddenly not being who and what he now knew her to be. They'd only had this knowledge for a short time, but it already felt so natural and right that he couldn't imagine the world in any other way. He reached out and touched the side of her face. "No, Lori. It's genetic, just like having beautiful brown eyes or a little mole near your jawline. It's how you're made."

She leaned ever so slightly into his palm and closed her eyes. When she opened them a moment later, Rex saw a mixture of sadness and determination. "All right, then. Let's go."

He brought her into the kitchen, suddenly conscious of how she might think about it. Would she be intimidated when she saw the industrial stove and the massive island that also served as a breakfast bar, understanding just how many people could be fed there? Would that make her realize how extensive the pack was? It could make her feel less alone or utterly terrified.

Rex took her hand and headed into the hallway. "We'll go to my den, where we can talk privately."

As he passed by the dining area, he caught a glimpse of Max and Brody playing cards with Caleb and Sean. Brody had actually set his pencils down long enough to hold a hand of cards. Max was glaring at his own, looking like he was about to lose. Rex gave his brothers a nod and moved on past them. Lori would end up getting introduced to everyone in time, but she was already overwhelmed as it was.

"I guess I should've asked if you were hungry before we left the kitchen," he said.

"I'm fine, really." Lori ducked her head from side to side as she glanced into the other rooms they passed.

"Rex." His brother's voice was deep and angry behind him.

"What's up?" If pack business needed to be discussed, or the guys wanted him to join them, it would just have to wait. Rex turned to address his brother.

Max still had his cards in his hands but pointed at Lori with his other one. "I don't understand. It was one thing to bring her back here in the first place. And I think I was pretty damn tolerant when you hired her at Selene's. But now you've brought her here again? What the hell is up with this?"

Rex immediately put himself between Lori and his brother. Max's eyes narrowed as he understood the gesture for exactly what it was. "Things are happening that you don't understand."

"Clearly, but I suggest you enlighten me. You're in charge of—" Max cut himself off with a growl, not wanting to give away their secrets to a human.

"It's all right. She knows." Rex could sense Lori behind him. Damn it! He should've taken the time to call ahead. She'd already been afraid to come there, and this just proved she'd been right. This wasn't how it was supposed to go down. She wasn't a human, but the others wouldn't know that until they got closer to her and could scent the difference.

"She knows?" Max repeated, his voice rising. "So Dawn's magic didn't work?"

"Magic?" Lori whispered to herself behind him. "Holy shit. As if wolves aren't enough."

Brody, Caleb, and Sean came out of the dining area to see what was happening. They were on alert, but at least they weren't ready to fly off the handle like Max.

Rex put his hands up to stave off any further questions. "It did work, but there's more to this. I'll explain it all to you in a bit, but right now, I've—"

"No." Max slapped his hand of cards into Caleb's chest. Startled, Caleb took them and slipped them into his back pocket as the beta stepped forward. "I've been patient. I've been trusting. Just like I'm supposed to be. I've been nothing but honest with you, and I think it's about damn time you were honest with the rest of us."

"I will be, but not right now," Rex returned,

finding that the more Max's frustration flared, so did his own. "I'm going to talk to everyone at once as soon as I take care of a few things. What's been happening here calls for an official meeting."

He was going to have one hell of a sore throat with all the talking he needed to do.

"No. I'm not waiting any longer. You've already stirred up too much tension in the pack. That's exactly why Dave has been such an asshole lately. There's no telling what he might do next." Max gestured wildly with his hands to suggest that the possibilities were endless.

Fine. If this was going to have to be the way it was, then so be it. "Like attack me? The way he did when Lori and I came out of Selene's tonight?"

Max's shoulders sagged, and the other three men glanced at each other in shock. "Are you shitting me?"

"No." No one had taken Dave's threats seriously other than Max, apparently, and it made Rex feel like a fool. Dave had warned him, but he never thought a ranking packmate would come at him with such a thorough betrayal. "We closed down and left a little early because Lori wasn't feeling good. Dave was waiting for us out there with Randy and Adam, and they attacked us."

Brody leaned against the wall and folded his arms in front of his chest. He eyed his older brother casually as though they were talking about nothing more consequential than the weather. "Dave's always been strong, and he wouldn't keep the others with him if they weren't, too. How did you manage to handle them by yourself?"

Rex blew out a breath. Son of a bitch. They were making this so much harder than it had to be. "He was too confident for one thing."

"And the other?" Max demanded.

He couldn't do this to her. He couldn't just tell everyone her secret right in front of her, especially since she hadn't yet had the chance to understand it all for herself. It would take time, but Rex knew he didn't have that right now. Sometimes, as an Alpha, there were things he had to do whether he wanted to or not. Turning to Lori, he pointed to the door at the end of the hall. "That's my den. Go on in there and make yourself comfortable. I'll join you after I've dealt with this."

Lori looked up at him, but then her eyes dashed to the other men who faced them. She made no move to do as he asked.

"Might as well just do what he says," Max

advised. "I'm tired of waiting, and he's obviously not going to tell me the truth while you're here."

Rex glared at his brother. "That's because it's not my truth to tell."

"What the hell is that supposed to mean?" Max demanded.

Lori closed her eyes. Her lashes rested softly against the skin just underneath them. Her lips puckered in for a moment and then came out again, newly pink. She flexed her hands against her thighs and then turned to look at Max. "It means he wasn't alone when he was fighting Dave."

"You don't have to do this," Rex said swiftly. He'd felt all her tension and uncertainty on the drive over, and it was high again as they faced members of his own pack who demanded to know what was happening. It wasn't fair, and he'd be damned if she had to come clean this way.

"Maybe I do." She closed her eyes again.

When her breath made her chest rise, Rex realized he was holding his. He watched in awe as her head rolled back. Her ears moved against her skull, forming familiar furry points. Her body lurched and jerked as she transitioned, her bones adjusting for her new shape. She slumped slightly against the wall as she fought to regain her balance.

Rex reached for her, but once she had all paws on the floor, she didn't need him. Her fur was thick and pure white, just as he'd seen it before. The awe he felt at seeing her in this form wasn't diminished by the circumstances surrounding them. His heart trembled, and his wolf cried out to be with her.

For now, he held himself at bay as Lori opened her violet eyes and gazed at the other shifters who had doubted her a moment ago.

14

Lori lifted her muzzle, waiting to see what would happen. She had no idea if there was any sort of protocol for when someone shifted into their other form. For all she knew, she'd just pissed everyone off. Well, so be it. She was pissed off, too, and Max needed to shut the hell up already.

The other shifters—or at least, so she assumed—let out cries of astonishment and a string of unintelligible questions. The blonde one just laughed and shook his head.

As for Max, he gaped at her for a long moment before his eyes finally lifted to Rex's. "Did you know?"

"No, not until tonight. Neither did she. It's all a bit complicated, which is why I needed you to just listen to me." Rex's fists curled and straightened at his sides.

Lori watched them, wondering just how much trouble she'd caused. At the same time, she couldn't deny just how good her wolf felt. When she'd stood just behind Rex a moment ago in her human form, her body wouldn't stop trembling as she'd worried about all the implications of her new identity. She felt like there was a threat around every corner, both physically and emotionally.

Now, she felt strong and steady as she stood in the narrow space of the hallway next to Rex. It wasn't simply because she had four feet on the ground instead of two, either. She could feel every muscle and every fiber of fur. The self-awareness was incredible, like being a teenager again, minus the zits and awkwardness. That was exactly why she'd attempted to jump into the fight against Dave, even though she had no experience and it was obvious the other wolf was going to do something drastic.

She could get addicted to this once she stopped being so scared of it.

"What's going on?" A door slammed somewhere else in the house.

An older man, his gray hair a tangled swoop on his forehead, adjusted his glasses as he came running into the hallway. He looked to Rex for an answer, but his head tipped back on his neck when he saw Lori. "Oh. My. Joan, you're going to want to see this."

"What is it?" Still fastening the belt on her long black robe, a woman crowded into the doorway next to him. Her long gray hair fell in curls around her, and the deep purple of her nails glowed as she spread her bony hand across her chest. She gasped as she looked from Lori to Rex and back again. "Rex, my dear. Who is this?"

Rex touched a finger to Lori's shoulder. "Lori, you might want to change back so I can officially introduce you to my parents."

"Lori? The human everyone was in an uproar about?" his mother asked as she stepped closer. She walked slowly, like someone trying not to spook a wild animal. Small crystals on a leather string around her neck softly tinkled together, and she brought the smell of lavender with her. "Incredible! And obviously not as human as everyone thought."

Even though Lori now understood she wasn't human, she couldn't help but be insulted. Dave had obviously been upset that she was human, something she hadn't caught onto before because she'd had no idea there was an alternative. She had a good notion that Max had felt the same way, and probably a few others.

"That's the one," Rex confirmed quietly.

"Don't change back yet, dear." The older woman knelt in front of Lori, admiring her like an exhibit in a museum. "You are absolutely magnificent. That fur, and those eyes! Right here in our very own packhouse!"

Rex cleared his throat, clearly embarrassed. "What are you talking about, Mom?"

Instead of answering, Joan just looked lovingly at Lori. "I'd like to try something. May I touch you?" She held her hands out, her fingers cupping the air.

There was something about this woman that Lori instantly liked. She was soft and genuine, someone who truly didn't care what other people thought, yet commanded their respect. Lori was pretty sure it didn't have anything to do with the fact that she was related to Rex. So was Max, and there was obviously no love lost there. Unable to speak like she was used to, Lori took a small step forward.

"Thank you." Joan placed her hands on either side of Lori's head. Her fingers were gentle as they moved deep down into her silky fur. "Now, close your eyes."

Lori did as she was told, though she was very

aware of just how many people were crowded into the hallway to see what was going on. Her sharp hearing detected more footsteps from other areas in the house, and for a moment, she thought about backing away. She should just change back into human form and speak. That was the type of communication she was used to, and even if she wasn't on the same level as these other shifters, it might make it easier for all of them.

But then, before she could truly make up her mind to do so, images began to flash before her eyes. They were too quick to keep track of at first, nothing more than shapes and colors dancing past her vision even though her eyes were shut tight. They intrigued her, but they were like butterflies that she couldn't catch. Lori no longer felt her body, neither her wolf nor her human form. She floated in a chaotic sea of color that she frantically tried to gain control of.

Suddenly, one of the pictures resolved itself. It wasn't a picture at all, but a scene from a party. The room was dark and smoky, the women in long dresses with their hair curled up on the backs of their heads and the men in tuxedos. The windows were purely black, showing how late this party was going. A woman in the center of the room played hostess, walking a tray of appetizers around and talking and laughing with her guests. She looked at Lori with a small smile playing on her lips, and her brown eyes turned a brilliant shade of violet.

Lori fell into them, caught in a cataract of amethyst. She plunged headfirst, seeing more of those flashing images all around her. She reached out and tried to touch one. Her hand felt the spark of electricity, and she dove into another scene.

A woman ran through a field illuminated by moonlight. She'd gathered her white dress up around her knees, and it glowed blue among the wheat. She looked over her shoulder at her pursuers. Their heavy boot steps echoed through the night and into Lori's bones. The woman ran into the woods, where the shadows of the trees fell like long stripes across a thick path. Lori felt her paws hitting the hard ground as she ran alongside her, sending up the fresh scent of pine needles as she passed through. The woman suddenly came to a stop in a clearing. Lori wanted to cry out to her to run, but all the fear and panic that'd been on the woman's face was gone as she lifted her arms to the full moon above her head. Complete darkness descended around them.

Lori swam in that darkness, completely alone now. A pinprick of light formed in the center. It grew closer and brighter until Lori could see a woman on a chariot. Two snowy white horses heaved against their harnesses as they drew the cart across the ground. A woman drove that chariot, one with a strong nose and a blunt chin. She wore a set of bull horns on her head, and a long, glittering cape streamed out behind her. Emotions overwhelmed Lori, even though the woman she saw didn't seem to be bothered in the least as she held her torch in front of her and called out a battle cry.

She wanted to see more, to know more, but something pulled her back. Lori resisted, wanting to stay. Everything was so beautiful, and it made her heart feel so deeply. But the force that dragged her back was stronger, insistent. A tunnel formed around her as she went. All of those brief images and scenes were still around her, teasing her, but they moved more slowly this time. Lori saw glimpses of numerous lives, of a woman smiling as she bathed her children, of lovers finally united, of wolves flowing down a mountainside like water. She felt herself in all of them, and she let out a cry of pain as it all slipped away from her and darkness took over once again.

"Come back to us, dear," a soft voice said. "We're waiting for you."

Slowly, Lori opened her eyes. A woman leaned over her, smiling sweetly. Lori blinked, thinking that she should recognize this woman's face even though she didn't. Another face was there, and this one she did know. "Rex?"

He let out a sharp breath and shook his head. "You really scared me there for a minute. I wasn't sure if you were okay."

Reality didn't feel quite right. Her ears were buzzing, and her body felt strange. She realized she was no longer in her wolf form at all. The things she'd just seen had felt so real, but they were quickly slipping further and further away. She felt the hard floor beneath her and the clothes on her body, material things that made everything else begin to fade like a dream. She remembered that the woman next to her in the black robe was Joan, and she recognized the other shifters who stood staring in wonder.

"It's all right." Rex smoothed a warm hand over her forehead. "Someone get her some water. And call Dawn."

"She'll be fine," his mother intoned softly as she laid a hand on Lori's cheek and smiled. "She's been on a long journey, that's all."

Lori swallowed as Rex helped her sit up, propping her against the wall but keeping a protective arm around her. "What did I just see? It all felt so real."

Joan smiled. "I'm sorry. I know you weren't quite prepared for that, but no one could be. You've traveled back through all of your other lives and those of your ancestors. There's more information there than you can imagine, but you saw the most important parts. You are a descendant of Selene herself."

Max had just returned with a cold bottle of water. The blood drained from his face. "Are you sure, Mom?"

"Oh, yes." Joan hadn't taken her hazel eyes off of Lori, but now she lifted them so that she gave Rex a knowing look. "She's special. So very special, indeed."

Rex's jaw hardened.

Lori accepted the cold water from Max. It helped her feel a little more real, but it didn't help any of this make sense. "Selene?"

Joan trailed her fingers in an arc through the air. "The goddess of the moon. There have been many other deities who represented the moon, but she is the moon herself. Our pack is devoted to her, which is where that old tale about werewolves and full moons came from, but it goes so much deeper than that."

"All the wolf packs were devoted to her, but many have fallen out of the practice," Rex explained quietly. He gently pushed a tendril of Lori's hair off of her forehead. "You could say that we're a little more traditional. I gave my club her name so that other wolves would know they were safe there."

"I never even thought about the name," Lori mumbled.

"You wouldn't have had any reason to," Joan assured her, "just as none of us would've had any reason to think you might be her descendent. But with that white fur and those violet eyes, I knew you were no ordinary wolf."

Lori wasn't sure there was any such thing as 'ordinary' now that she knew about shifters, a moon goddess, and past lives. "It was like I was there. I saw so many things, but I saw *her*. She was so incredibly powerful." Lori longed to get that feeling back again as she watched Selene urge her chariot forward.

"And so are you, in your own way," Joan said with a smile.

"Listen, Lori." Max ran a hand through his dark hair. "I'm really sorry. I shouldn't have treated you the way I did. I had no idea. But that's not an excuse. I was a real ass."

She looked up at him. Not all that long ago, she'd

been annoyed with Max for being pissy with her and questioning Rex's motives. Now, after having taken a trip that expanded far beyond the time and space of an entire lifetime, Lori found that she didn't really mind at all. "Don't worry about it. It's no big deal."

"But it is," Max argued. "I want to make it up to you. You just say the word, and I'll do it."

"I think that's enough groveling for now." Rex stood and helped Lori to her feet. "I need to get her someplace a little more comfortable than the floor, if you don't mind. I'm sure we'll all get a chance to talk again later."

Thinking once again of those strong, radiant women, Lori felt silly having to lean against Rex just to walk down a hallway. "How did I get to the floor, anyway?"

He kept his right arm around her waist and held her left hand with his. "My mother opened up a vision for you. As if you don't have enough things to think about, she's a witch as well as a wolf. It pulled you into a deeper consciousness, and your body couldn't handle it. You essentially passed out and shifted back."

"Oh. At least I didn't have to feel the pain this time." Changing from one form to another was excruciating, but at least the agony didn't last once the deed was done.

Rex opened the door at the end of the hallway to reveal a cozy den. Solid wood bookshelves lined the walls, though one was being used as an entertainment center with a flat-screen TV. The long window on the side of the room probably let in a lot of light in the mornings, but right now, it was so solidly dark, it could've been painted. A fireplace crackled opposite it. He closed the door and brought her to a long leather couch on the right.

"I know you've got to be exhausted, but we have so much to talk about."

15

"Would you like a drink?" Rex sure as hell knew he could use one as he stepped over to the bar cart in the corner. "The stuff I keep here is better than what you'll find at the club."

"Um, yeah. I think I will." Lori sank back into the sofa and closed her eyes. "Have you ever been so tired, you thought you might never be able to fall asleep again?"

He poured two glasses of bourbon, neat, and brought them around to the sofa. He took a sip of his before putting it on the coffee table in front of him, noting the way Lori frowned down into her glass. "I have. I think I might be getting there right now. If you'd like, I could make arrangements for you to stay the night, and we can talk about this in the morning."

The truth was he didn't want to wait, although he would if she asked him to. Many things in his life hadn't made sense over the last few weeks, but that night, they'd coalesced into a picture he could see with remarkable clarity. Rex wanted her to feel the same.

"No." She took a slow drink and then frowned into her glass again. "There's a lot I still need to know, and I don't think my brain will shut off until I get some of those answers. Besides, I've inconvenienced you enough."

"Not in the slightest. It's been a strange night, but it's not an inconvenience, nor your fault." He picked up his drink again and forced his eyes away from her. It felt like he was staring. Who could blame him, considering what he'd found in her? And as for spending the night, well, both sides of him would've been more than happy to know that Lori was under his roof for the night. Even better if she were in his bed.

He cleared his throat. That would have to wait until later.

"If you say so. You already ended up banishing three members of your pack, which includes two of your employees. Your brother was so pissed off that I thought he might hit the roof, and we woke the whole house up. I still don't quite understand everything about this whole descended-from-Selene, thing, but that seemed to cause quite a stir."

"Sounds like an average night at the packhouse," he said with a smile. "Let's get these boots off you. You should be more comfortable." Without giving her a chance to protest, he took her heel and pulled the laces. She was still wearing her thick winter socks underneath them by the time he set the boots near the fireplace, but a shiver of intimacy warmed his spine.

She tucked her sock feet underneath her. "Your mom seems nice."

Rex resumed his place next to her on the couch. That was the sort of thing someone would say after meeting their boyfriend's parents for the first time at the Olive Garden. Lori's first encounter with Joan Glenwood had been entirely different, yet Rex thought it just might serve as the launching point he needed. There was so much to say, and it was hard to know where to start. "She is. She's also very talented. She serves as the oracle of our pack, a spiritual leader who offers all the information within her power."

Lori eyed him cautiously. "This isn't a cult or something, is it? Because I'm not into that."

Rex laughed despite how nervous she was making him. "No. Not a cult. Centuries of tradition, plus being lucky enough that my mother comes from a family of witches, but not a cult."

She laughed, too, though it was a tired one. "Okay then. I guess that's good."

He pressed his lips together and forced himself back on track. The clock above the mantel ticked loudly, mocking him for how long it was taking him to get around to this. "She has the ability to see into the future, although if you ever ask her to do a tarot reading for you, she'll start by reminding you that you have your own free will. Things aren't always set in stone."

"Makes sense to me." She was watching him carefully, waiting.

Of course she was. He'd brought her in there to talk privately, when she'd already learned about shifters, packs, magic, and powerful ancestors. What could possibly be more important than that?

"She's told me for a long time that I would find someone very special," he continued. "I didn't know exactly what that meant, and it took long enough to happen that I was starting to think it never would. Then you came along."

"How do you know she meant me?" Lori asked. "I heard her say I was special, but couldn't there be others?"

She wasn't going to make this easy, but it hadn't been up until now, anyway. Rex scooted a little closer to her on the couch and laid his hand over hers. "Lori, shifters aren't like humans. We don't just fall in love with someone we're attracted to and decide to get married. It's not that random. We believe there's only one other person for us, a true soulmate. It's like finding the other half of ourselves that we've been missing, and we're never really complete until we find that person. Sometimes it takes the universe a long time to bring us together."

The deep chestnut of her eyes was steady on him. "Are you saying you think we're meant to be together?"

"I know we are," he affirmed. "I can feel it inside me everytime I'm near you. I felt it from the very beginning, but I was in denial because I thought you were human. I can see now how stupid that was. I shouldn't have had to wait until I knew your truth, and I'm sorry for that. But the wolf inside me has been calling out to you all this time, and I know you can feel yours doing the same."

Tiny muscles twitched in her face as she tried to take it all in. She turned her hand over and curled her fingers around his. "I do feel that," she whispered. "I guess that's been my wolf the whole time, but I didn't know it until today. I'd never felt it before, and I didn't know how to identify it or explain it. I guess I thought I was just changing because of everything that's happened in my life lately. You know, when you think about it, I really was."

Rex felt warm inside as he heard her laugh at the end of that. She'd been through so much, and it gave him hope that they would come out on the other side of this intact. "I never would've imagined you could possibly be more gorgeous than you already were." He wrapped his arms around her and pulled her close, pressing his lips gently to hers.

She returned the gesture, her lips warm and soft. Not demanding or primal this time, as things had been before between them. That would come again, but now, it was a different kind of need, one of comfort and tranquility.

Rex brushed his hand through her hair as he pulled back and looked at her. "I've waited my whole life for you, my Luna, and now I can finally be home."

"Luna?" she asked as she settled in against his shoulder.

He could close his eyes and just sit there forever, enjoying the feel of her at his side. "Since I'm the Alpha, my mate is called the Luna. If you accept the bond between us, you'll allow me to mark you."

Lori pulled back, her eyes quizzical. "Mark me? What do you mean?"

"A gentle bite. Right there." He touched the bit of muscle between her shoulder and her neck, the skin warm beneath his finger. The idea of it sent a thrill coursing through his veins, and his fangs threatened to descend. Rex held them back, knowing that even if Lori agreed to it, she probably wouldn't do so tonight. "All shifters used to do this, but over time, it's become a lost practice. Our pack continued to uphold the tradition, though, based on the guidance Selene had passed down to our oracles over generations. After marking, physical mating will solidify our bond and allows us to feel each other's deepest emotions. Nothing can come between us."

She pushed herself further back, making him open his arms to give her space. "This is more intense than I realized."

"Very," he agreed, and he could feel his lust for her building the longer they discussed it. Rex's wolf was thrashing inside of him, reminding him just how much he wanted to dive into her soul and her mind. "Mates are meant to be together in every way possible. Do you remember that we could speak to each other telepathically when we were both in wolf form?"

Shock registered on her face. "I guess we did. I was a little preoccupied and didn't think about it much."

"Because it was so natural," he chuckled. Unable to completely resist her, he leaned down and touched his lips to her neck. "We get to take that and move it to an even deeper level. It'll be important for us as we run the pack together."

"I may know how to run a saloon, but I don't know a damn thing about running a pack of wolves," she protested softly as she tipped her head back to give him better access.

He kissed the hollow of her collarbone, and though the thought of marking her tempted him, he knew there was plenty more to keep him occupied. "The Luna is like the pack mother. She ensures that everyone in the pack is taken care of. She runs the packhouse, helps care for those in need, gives advice, and collaborates with me on decisions affecting the pack. Things like that."

"Hold on a second." She stiffened underneath him and pushed back, breaking him out of the reveries of kissing her soft skin and inhaling her sweet scent. "This sounds an awful lot like a job."

Rex's heart was still thundering, but not because he was turned on. In that one second, he realized she was slipping away from him. He'd found her, and she was just as special as he'd always been promised, but that didn't mean he was going to get to keep her. "You don't have to think about it like that. It's just a natural one; one that you were born for. For me, the club is my job, but the pack is my destiny. As are you."

Lori turned away from him, tapping her fingers against the leather arm of the couch. "I think I might've been wrong when I said I wanted to know everything."

"It's not like everything has to change in one night." He touched his fingers to her chin and turned her toward him. "All we have to do for the moment is be together. Everything else will come naturally."

She tipped her head back to lift herself out of his grip, though she still looked at him. "It's kind of romantic to talk about how we're meant to be. I can't say I'm really even turned off by the whole marking thing, considering I already nipped you a little when I didn't even know that was a thing. But I don't know about the rest of it. I can't have people relying on me when I'm not even sure I can rely on myself right now."

"You're being too hard on yourself." How could he make her understand? "It's new, and it feels like a big challenge, but it'll only get easier. Your shifting will get quicker and less painful. When you move in, you'll start to see the way the packhouse runs and how our dynamics work. Don't think of it as some big lesson or training for a new job. We'll take it one day at a time. Together. As we're meant to."

"It's just not sitting well with me. When I moved from Chinook, I was scrambling to get my life back together. I felt like I'd started over completely and would never catch up again. Once I got my apartment and a job, I thought maybe I wasn't doing that bad after all. But then this wolf thing happened, and it doesn't make sense because no one in my family ever mentioned a damn thing about wolves."

"Sometimes the trait is latent," Rex explained quietly, trying to imagine how it would be to suddenly have news like this. He'd always been a wolf for as long as he could remember. "There are even shifters who have the genes and can pass them on but can't use them for themselves. There was a wolf somewhere down the line, but if no one had shifted in a few generations, the information might not have been passed down. That's provided anyone knew in the first place. Like I said, we're pretty secretive."

She pressed her fingers into her temples and rotated them slowly. "However it happened, it's a lot. I know I keep saying that, but I don't know how else to express it. Then your mother tells me I'm descended from a goddess, and you tell me I'm destined to be with you. But that's not enough, is it? I'm supposed to be in charge of a whole pack of wolves, most of whom want nothing to do with me."

Rex hadn't liked it when the others had protested her presence before, but that was when they'd thought she was human. Now that he understood she was his mate, Rex instantly felt his chest burn with anger. "That's not true. They'll have full respect for you. Even now, I'm sure word of your true heritage is spreading like wildfire through the pack. That's enough, but once they know who you are to me, there'll be absolutely no question."

She stopped rubbing her temples, and her eyes flew open. "Conner."

Lori had mentioned her son regularly when they were at work.

"What if this is something that he has, too?" she asked desperately.

"I suppose that would depend on what got passed down from his father's side, plus how strong your own shifter trait is. There's no clear measure of that, though. As I'm sure you can imagine, we don't exactly have all the scientific answers."

Lori leaned heavily on the arm of the couch. "It's hard enough to talk to your kid about puberty, sex, and drugs, but wolves? He'll think I'm insane."

"Not if you show him the way you did Max," Rex pointed out, still finding the memory of his beta's shocked face rather amusing. The way he'd practically knelt before her had only added to the effect. "That worked rather well."

"It's not funny. At least he already knew shifters exist," Lori pointed out.

"You're right. I'm sorry. I'm not trying to make light of this. I just don't want you to feel like this is impossible." Over his forty-five years, Rex had often envisioned what it would be like to find his mate, and in that fantasy he'd imagined they'd both know and understand their connection so deeply, there'd be no question of it. Now, with despair all over Lori's face, he wasn't entirely sure. "I'm here to help you get through this. So is the rest of the pack."

"Right. The pack I'm supposed to take care of when I don't even know how to take care of myself." Lori pushed herself to her feet. "Rex, I need to go home."

He rested his hands on her hips and pulled her close. "I don't want to leave you when you feel like this. I know I'm a constant reminder of this new information, but I do believe that the two of us are meant to be together. You're my Luna."

She rested her forehead against his shoulder, and Rex felt himself relax as she leaned into him. "I don't know if I can be that."

He closed his eyes. Rex had waited so long, long enough that he'd thought it might never happen for him. Here was his mate, an incredible, irresistible woman. She was a part of him, but he couldn't make her stay. He could only hope that once he'd let her go, she'd decide to come back to him. "I'll take you home."

16

"YOU'VE BEEN A GREAT AUDIENCE! COME BACK NEXT Saturday night and see us again. That'll be our last concert for a while before we hit the studio. Thank you and good night!"

The audience exploded with cheers, rocking Rex back into the present moment. He shook himself, wondering how long he'd been standing there like a zombie. Selene's was packed with people. He knew he'd been taking orders and making drinks, and that Max had been working the floor, but he didn't remember any of it. His mind had been elsewhere.

Glancing up to see a patron signal to him for another beer, Rex grabbed a mug and pulled the tap. How could he have let Lori go like that? He had to, he knew. He didn't want her to feel obligated toward him, even though their souls knew what should happen. Rex wanted Lori to *want* to be with him. How had that never occurred to him before when he'd dreamed of finally finding his mate?

Foam spilled over his hand. Rex cursed and set the mug down to clean up the mess. He mopped it up with a rag and handed the drink to the waiting customer.

"You all right?" Max came up behind him to mix a martini.

"Yeah," Rex grunted. He wasn't at all, and he wasn't sure he would be again, but that was just the way it was. It didn't mean that he wanted to talk about it.

His brother eyed him as he grabbed the vodka. "That's hard to believe, considering everything else."

Rex rolled a shoulder. "It is what it is."

Max was quiet for a bit as he shook the drink and strained it into a cocktail glass. "For what it's worth, I'm sorry for my role in all of it."

There was no doubt that Max's attitude toward Lori hadn't helped, but Rex didn't blame him. Dave had threatened their very lives and put the pack in danger, but even that wasn't the problem right now. He could change all that, but it wouldn't necessarily make Lori come back to him. "It's not your fault."

Carefully placing the olives on a toothpick and plopping it into the drink, Max shrugged. "Maybe not, but I still don't like it for you. And I plan to apologize to her about a thousand more times."

"I hope she gives you the chance to."

The band was breaking down, and the two brothers began the closing routine. Rex was on autopilot, just as he'd been ever since he'd taken Lori home. His heart had shattered as he'd walked her to her door, insisting to himself he was doing it for her safety and not just because he didn't want to let her go. Rex had explained he'd stationed some guards nearby to ensure there was no threat from Dave, and she accepted that well enough. He'd restrained himself from trying to convince her that this was the right path for her, although now he wished he had.

The garage door was open when he rolled in, spilling a rectangle of light out into the driveway. Johnny Cash pumped through the night air amidst the sound of metal clanging against metal. Several tool carts had been pulled away from the walls and were spread around the concrete, along with a few car parts.

Leaving his truck in the driveway, Rex walked up to see his father bent under the hood of an old red car. Or at least, it'd been red at one time. The paint was faded and chipped. "What heap of junk are you working on now?"

Jimmy straightened and smiled. He ran a self-conscious hand through his hair, something that had always been his pride and joy back when he was younger and it was darker. "This is no heap of junk! It's a 1957 Chevrolet Bel Air sport coupe. This is my dream car."

"Looks more like a nightmare." As Rex smiled, he could feel just how tired he was in his face. The nights had been long and fitful, full of flashes of dreams and uncomfortable thoughts. Even a long run through the woods behind the packhouse didn't wear him out enough. Spending time in that form and exploring the natural state of things usually felt cathartic, but he was left just as numb as he'd been before.

Crossing the garage to turn down the volume on his Best Hits of the Fifties cassette, his father grinned. "I guess it does at the moment, but trust me, this is exactly what I've always wanted. This is the car of my childhood and early teen years, a representation of freedom and excitement that I could never afford until now."

Rex peered under the hood. He knew a little

about cars. There was no avoiding it growing up around Jimmy, considering it'd always been his passion. He didn't need any of that knowledge to see that this car would need a ton of work. "I'm guessing the literal squirrel's nest under here probably had something to do with the discount."

"Probably," he agreed with a smile. "That's all right. You know, the way this pack has been run recently means that every one of our members has what they need. When I was growing up, we didn't even have that. I'd dreamed of a car like this, but I knew a long time ago that I had to set that dream aside because it wasn't going to happen. I never really forgot about it, though."

Rex walked around the back to examine the tail fins. Even in its current state, the car was the epitome of its era. He could see the appeal, though it wasn't something he would go after himself. Newer vehicles with all of the accommodations were more his style. "I guess our dreams don't always come true."

"I like to think they do eventually if we're patient enough. The proof is right here." Jimmy picked up a wrench and bent under the hood again, cracking a loose, rusted bolt and dropping it into an old coffee can. "Those dreams don't always come to us the way we think they will, but when a buddy offered me this as a trade, I just couldn't resist."

The garage was a roomy one since his father had added onto it a few years ago. The back part housed the cars already in Jimmy's collection, ones that he'd meticulously restored down to having the right nuts and bolts. They were bright and shiny compared to what he was working on now. "It's not even a convertible."

"Your mother likes the wind in her hair in the moment, but not when she's brushing all the knots out later." A second rusty bolt went in after the first one.

"I don't know why you like these things. They're not much compared to the new vehicles rolling off the assembly line." Noticing that the rust on the next bolt wasn't giving way, Rex grabbed the can of WD-40 and handed it over.

His father nodded his appreciation. "GPS and rear cameras are nice and all, but you might be surprised at what kind of options were available on the fifty-seven. Power windows, power seats, even air conditioning. There was a speaker in the back for surround sound, and you could even get auto-dimming headlights."

"You're shitting me. Half the models you have in

here don't even have power steering." Rex easily
remembered the first time Jimmy had let him
behind the wheel of one of his vintage cars. He was
young, and he'd only learned to drive on newer
models. He'd gotten used to it eventually, but they
weren't for everyone.

"I shit you not. You could even get an electric
shaver that went with it. Of course, there were some
downsides, too. You see that piece of plastic there
just behind the windshield?" He gestured around
the open hood, pointing toward the driver's seat.

Rex looked, seeing a fan-shaped piece of ribbed
plastic that had definitely seen better days. "Yeah."

Jimmy kept working as he talked, slowly pulling
out a large metal cowl. "Well, the roofline of the car
extends out real far. It looks pretty, but it means you
can't see the traffic lights when you're driving. So you
just look at that little piece of plastic, which reflects
the color of the lights."

"Real safe," Rex mumbled. "You'd think with
everything else they offered they could've worked on
that a little."

"Times were different. Hand me a couple of
gloves out of that box, will you? I don't think
anything is still living under here anymore, but I
want to be safe."

Fetching the nitrile gloves and wheeling over a trash can, Rex found a dustpan and a hand broom to help with the process. Leaves, pine needles, nuts, and scraps of paper came tumbling out of the car. Some fell through and scattered on the floor. "And you still want it even though it's in this condition?"

"Like I said, it was my dream. It finally came to me, so I'm going to take it," he replied simply as he dumped a big handful of debris into the barrel. "I might have to spend some time to get it where I want it to be, but it'll be worth it in the end."

A car was a simple enough dream. At one point, when he was much younger, Rex had dreamed of cars, too. The model depended on which one was currently displayed on his wall calendar or what some other guy happened to drive into the high school parking lot. Music had been more of his thing, and he'd already managed to make that a massive part of his life. That hollow area was still inside him, though, one he'd momentarily thought was finally filled. "So what happens when your dream finally comes to you, and you're not sure you'll get to keep it after all?"

Jimmy used his shoulder to adjust his glasses. "Now I know we're not talking about cars anymore because this car isn't going anywhere. I take it things haven't progressed with Lori?"

"No." Having reached everything they could from the top, Rex started sweeping up what had fallen on the floor. "I can't even decide if I ought to call her or just let her have the space to think. She was so burdened by everything that happened that night. She told me so many times that it was too much. I understand that it was in the moment, but I worry that she won't stop thinking that way."

"Mmhm." Jimmy nodded as he moved around past the headlight and tugged on a wire. It popped loose instantly, and he laid it aside on a nearby worktable. "You know, I wasn't sure things would work out when I met your mother."

Having grown up seeing his parents constantly groping each other, that was hard to believe. "You don't have to make stuff up just to make me feel better. I know everyone must think I'm a failure for not being able to keep his mate."

Pulling off his gloves and chucking them in the trash can, his father leaned against the car and gave him a look from the other side of the raised hood. "First of all, I'm not making a damn thing up. Second, no one thinks that."

"She left the same night that we realized what we were to each other," Rex countered.

"That doesn't mean she's gone forever, son. Hell, if I thought Joan was gone for good every time she got overwhelmed and walked away for a little while, I would've spent half my life brokenhearted." He reached behind him for a screwdriver and began disassembling the headlight. The lens was cracked, but another was already laid out on top of a toolbox.

"Really?"

"Oh, hell yeah. Life is crazy, and it tends to throw a lot of shit our way all at once. We all need a little time to wrap our brains around it and figure out how to handle it. Your mother's favorite way to do that was to go off into the woods with her coven. Sometimes it was for an afternoon, sometimes for a week. At first, I got a little offended. I figured if we were mates, she should be with me while she worked all this out. But she needed her sisters, and she always came back to me. I just needed to have a little bit of faith that she would. Damn, I wonder how long this car was sitting outside."

Rex smiled at his father's acknowledgment that the car was a bit of a pain. "I guess I've been thinking about Lori the same way. I've known all my life that I'm a shifter, and I've understood the role of the

Alpha and the Luna. She should be here with me, talking about it, asking questions. If she's just at home trying to mull it all over on her own, she'll never understand it.

"But she needs to be *ready* to understand it," Jimmy pointed out. He cursed softly as the screw came out and fell to the floor somewhere under the car. "You think I was ready to understand that your mother was a witch? A powerful one, too. It intimidated the hell out of me, even as an Alpha. I knew she had a strong attachment to her pack, maybe even stronger than what most feel. I didn't know if I could really understand her, and I worried that coming to me wouldn't be enough for her. Your Lori isn't a witch, and she's only recently found out she's a wolf, but I'm sure there are all sorts of thoughts like that bouncing around in her head right now."

Which was exactly why she needed to be at the packhouse with Rex. "I guess you guys figured it out."

"Sure, we did."

"So what's the secret?"

"Lots of sex."

"Dad! I don't want to hear that!" Rex pinched the bridge of his nose, wondering if his father would ever really grow up.

Jimmy laughed. "I was young once, and so were you! There's not much more than that on a man's mind for most of his life, and you know it. But really, it does make a difference. There's a kind of connection that comes from it when things are right."

Well, Rex couldn't deny the truth in that, even if it was awkward to hear it from his own father. "I'd have to actually get close enough to touch her for that. Mom always said that my mate would be someone very special. She was right about that, but I thought that meant it would all be a lot easier."

"There's never a guarantee of that." Jimmy fiddled with the headlight assembly, no doubt wondering which pieces he might be able to salvage for another project. "We shifters talk about finding our mates as though it's this instantaneous thing, this magic spell that just slams into us and never lets go. Sure, it probably works out that way for some folks, but not all the time. We all still have human sides that have to be dealt with, don't forget. Just because you're destined to be together doesn't mean it's destined to be easy."

It'd been a long time since Rex had to ask his father for help. He was forty-five years old and at a point when he figured his parents probably needed *his* help more than the other way around. Even something as big as running the pack was just second nature to him, but it turned out there were problems he still needed his father for. "What do I do, Dad?"

"Well." Jimmy took the support out from under the hood and gently let it fall to a close. He crossed his arms in front of his chest and leaned against the grille. "She asked you for space. That's a test, even though I doubt she meant it that way. Are you going to be the kind of man who gives her what she asks for, or the kind of man who does what he wants?"

Rex let out a wry laugh. "I think I'd like to be both."

His dad smiled. "Personally, I think that's the right answer. Women love their men, but many of them seem to want time alone to do their own thing. We're the same way, even if we don't realize it. So give her time to think. Let her settle all of this in her brain. If some time has gone by and you haven't heard from her, remind her that you're still around, waiting for her. Then give her space again. Back and forth, it's the dance that men and women have been doing for ages."

"That's funny because I thought back in your day, the guy who won the rumble or the drag race was the one who got to take the girl home," Rex cracked.

"Sure. That, too," Jimmy said with a smile. "Don't worry about it too much, Rex. Things have a way of falling into place and happening as they're supposed to."

They closed the garage door, shut off the lights, and headed into the house. Rex sure hoped he was right.

17

LORI STARED AT HER LAPTOP SCREEN. SEVERAL TABS were open at the top, displaying every job search website she'd been able to think of. She'd scrolled through most of the results, even though she didn't remember the details of most of them. They either wanted more education than she had, the pay was too little to be worth her time, or she didn't have the right skills.

With a heavy sigh, she closed the laptop and pressed her hands over her eyes. Much bigger issues were at stake than her paycheck, but she'd thought looking for a new position would at least distract her enough to give her brain a break. It hadn't worked, and it just stressed her out more. She had some major life decisions to make but not enough information to base them on, and now she needed to worry about money on top of that. Life was grand.

She went into the kitchen and grabbed a glass from the cabinet. She wanted a big glass of soda, something terrible for her that she shouldn't have, but for the moment, she had to settle for juice. What would happen, she wondered as she filled her glass almost to the rim, if she decided to go back to Rex and accept this Luna thing? He'd made it sound so easy, as if she could just do it without thinking. Maybe he could, but she was still much more human than shifter. She didn't know a damn thing about wolf packs beyond what she'd seen on National Geographic.

On a whim, Lori went back to her computer and typed in a few other searches. No matter what keywords she used, she only found information about actual wolves or fictional characters. Rex hadn't been kidding when he'd said they were a secretive bunch. None of them had been crazy enough to put the truth on the internet. These days, that was saying something.

Restless and impatient with herself, she once again set the laptop aside. Lori crossed the room to the window and stared out at the gray day. Rex had said something about sending his pack members to keep an eye on her. The thought was both comforting and unsettling. She sure didn't want Dave to come back looking for revenge, but that didn't mean she was entirely at ease with some other guy watching her home. For a moment, she allowed herself to fantasize that Rex himself had come to keep her safe. The illusion was shattered instantly when she remembered that she couldn't just be a shifter, and she couldn't just be with Rex. She had to be something *more.*

Lori had already been more. She'd been a wife, a mom, and the co-owner of a saloon. Did being Rex's Luna mean she'd have to start all of those responsibilities over again, right when she was finding a sliver of freedom and time to herself? Or would enough benefits be in place to make it worth it? She wished she could call Abbie, but even her best friend wouldn't understand this predicament.

She realized there was one person she could call. Someone she *should* call, given what she knew now. Lori had been putting it off, terrified of the idea, but she could only wait so long. With shaking hands, she picked up her phone.

"Hey, Mom. What's up?" Conner's voice was too happy. But of course, he didn't know there was any reason to worry.

"Hi, honey. I, um, I just wanted to call and check in on you." Lori sat on the couch and pressed the phone to her ear.

"I'm fine. I just finished some homework, and I think all of my classes this semester are going to be a breeze."

"That's great, honey." She clenched her free hand. Every muscle in her body was tensed. Normally, if they were chatting on the phone, she'd go wash dishes or sweep the floor. Maybe the phone was the problem, though. "I was wondering if you'd want to come over this afternoon."

"Today?"

"Yeah. If you're free. No problem if you're not."

"Mom, are you all right? You sound a little edgy. Actually, you've sounded that way a lot lately."

And was it any wonder, considering a wild animal inside her had been trying to come out all this time? "I've been a little tense, I guess, but I'm fine."

He wasn't buying the lie. "I'm coming over. I'll be there in a few."

"Okay." She couldn't feel relieved when she hung up because now it meant she had to do it in person. That was the right thing. Lori knew that, but it was going to be harder. She had the pleasure of telling

him not only big news, but news she barely understood herself.

Conner had been honest when he'd said he'd be
over in a few. The knock on her door came quickly
enough that it startled her. To be sure, Lori checked
the peephole before opening the door. "Hey, honey."

"Hey." Conner studied her face as he came in. He
shut the door behind him and squinted down at her.
"Tell me what's really going on."

"Why do you think anything is going on?" she
hedged.

"I might be a lot younger than you, Mom, but I'm
not stupid. Something's bothering you. A lot. You've
got huge bags under your eyes, and you're also still
wearing your pajama pants. The only time I've seen
you do that this late in the day is when you're sick."

"Well, I'm not sick." She turned and stepped into
the living room, wishing she'd thought to change
clothes before he'd come over. With such a heavy
weight on her mind, she'd been lucky just to feed
herself. "I have been a little strange, though."

Conner eased himself down onto the couch,
sitting across from her. He leaned forward, bracing
his elbows on his knees. "Strange, how? Is this about
the menopause stuff again?"

"No, not that." He had a way of making her smile

in even the worst situations. Conner didn't even know he had that ability, but she was grateful for it.

"What is it then?"

Lori licked her lips. How could she tell her son she was a wolf? Furthermore, how could she tell him he could be one, too? This was so unfair. She'd already pretty much raised Conner by herself, considering how little Chuck had helped. Being a mom was challenging, but it shouldn't feel hard now that he was grown. These doubts only made her second-guess the idea of being Rex's Luna even more, but that wasn't the point at the moment. She was a wolf whether she was with Rex or not. "I don't quite feel like myself, I guess you could say. Do you ever feel like there's another part of you that you don't really let out?"

He sat up a little straighter. "Sure."

"And maybe you've had this other part of you buried so deeply within yourself that you didn't even realize it was there. But then life and everything else changes, and suddenly you start to wonder if the rest of your life has been a lie." Knowing what she was had certainly made her wonder how different the first four decades of her life would've been if she'd known.

Conner pressed his lips together, looking

serious. "You know, I'm taking a lot of generals this year. One of them is psychology. We've talked about all sorts of things, and this girl presented a paper about what happens to people when they get divorced. I thought the class was going to be boring, but this was actually pretty interesting. From what she said, it's really common for divorced people to try to live out all the things they didn't get to do when they were younger."

It was rewarding to know he was learning from his classes, but it wasn't getting her anywhere. "This doesn't really have anything to do with the divorce, but thank you. I guess I'm just trying to say that we don't always know everything about ourselves. We continue to learn and grow even as we get older. It can be a little strange sometimes."

Hell! Why couldn't she just come right out and say it?

"Mom." Conner got up and came to sit next to her on the loveseat. "I think I know what you're trying to tell me."

She touched his cheek. Grown though he was, he was still her baby boy. Was it going to break his heart to find out his mother wasn't human? How many sleepless nights would he have to spend wondering about his own identity? "You couldn't possibly, and I'm not doing a very good job of it."

"Give me a chance." Extending his arms out in front of him, Conner took a deep breath. As he let it out, the fine blonde hairs on the backs of his fingers thickened and turned white. His fingers receded, and his nails rounded into claws. Conner turned one paw over to show the dark pads underneath.

Lori's shriek split the air in the room. She scooted away from Conner, but only so she could face him. She reached out, holding his paws as they easily turned back into human hands. "Conner! You... you're..." Lori knew exactly what she'd seen, and she'd gone through it herself, but she still didn't know how to put it all into words.

"I'm sorry to scare you, Mom. I didn't know how to say it, but I did know how to show you." He patted his hands against his thighs. "I kind of thought that might be what you were getting at."

"It was. It was, honey."

He bent his head down so he could look into her face. "Mom? Are you...?"

She knew what he meant, even if he didn't say it. Lori nodded. "I am, but I only just found out. If you want me to prove it to you, you'd have to see the whole thing. It isn't pretty, and it turns out I'm not much of an indoor dog. I broke a few things when I tried it on my own."

Conner laughed, a sound she cherished, considering the current state of affairs. "Do you remember that vase that you used to keep on the coffee table? The pink one with the little bumps all over it?"

"Of course. It was a Fenton hobnail vase that my great aunt gave me. You broke it while throwing a baseball around in the living room." She hadn't thought about it for a long time.

"No. I broke it when I was running around the living room on four legs," he corrected with a bashful smile.

"I never really liked it anyway," she admitted, but the true weight of what he'd just said hit her hard. "Wait. How long have you been dealing with this?"

He rolled his eyes up toward the ceiling. "About five years, I guess. What took you so long?"

It was all so strange and silly that she had to laugh. "I don't know! It just happened. I think it might've had to do with a few other things, but we can go into that later. Tell me more about you, baby. I never imagined."

"All right. Let's see." He scratched the side of his nose. "You remember Austin Phillips? He'd always picked on me. I brushed him off for the longest time, just like you said. But it got worse in high school. It went from calling me names to trying to start fights with me. All the teachers said you should just ignore bullies, and they'll go away. Austin wasn't like that, and he followed me home one day after school. I knew what he was doing, so I cut through the park to get home faster. But he ran up on me and slugged me in the back of the head. The whole world went black, and I threw up. I thought I was dying. Instead, I changed into a wolf. I didn't even get the chance to go after Austin, because it scared the hell out of him. Needless to say, he was really nice to me after that and never said a word about it."

Her heart ached as she listened to his story. "Honey, why didn't you tell me any of this?"

Conner lifted his hands in defeat. "I think you know just how hard that is."

"I do." Tears stung the backs of her eyes, and her throat thickened. Lori leaned her head on Conner's shoulder. "What did you do, though? How have you been living with this?"

"I have good days and bad days if I'm honest. Sometimes I just live my life like a normal human being, and it doesn't matter. Other times, I don't know how I'll ever get used to this thing being a part of me. I can't talk about it. Mostly, I just throw myself into football and pretend I'm normal."

"Sweetheart." So many times, Lori had comforted Conner after a fall on the playground or a disappointment. She knew how to handle those. "I wish I knew what to say or how to help. I hate that you've had to go through this alone."

"Don't worry about it," he pointed out, one side of his mouth quirking up. "We can figure it out together."

"Yeah. There's still a lot I'm trying to figure out, but I can tell you that we're definitely not alone. There are a lot of shifters, and quite a few around here. I happened to be with one of them the first time my wolf came out."

Now it was his turn to be shocked. "Really? I always thought there had to be others, but I didn't know how to find them."

Her guts twisted, hoping her limited knowledge wouldn't be too much of a letdown for him. "I can't say for sure."

"What happened?" His dark eyes shimmered with excitement.

She'd thought it would be impossible to talk to someone else about what she'd gone through, but Lori had seen for herself that Conner had the same genes she did. She told him about Dave's threats, noticing the way her son's cheeks flushed with anger at hearing how he'd treated her. She went on to explain that she'd figured out why she wasn't feeling good, and that it'd resolved when Dave had ambushed them in the parking lot. "I guess, in a way, it was similar to what you experienced. I was so emotional. I was worried about Rex, and of course, I was scared for myself. I was angry with Dave for being such an ass, and it just happened. They were just as surprised as I was."

"That's pretty badass, Mom. I wish I'd been there to see it."

As big of a deal as that had been, it wasn't all of it. "Since Rex is a shifter, too, I had someone who could tell me what was happening. It helped, but it was too much information. Maybe I should get us each something to drink."

He put his hand on her knee to keep her from getting up. "I'll get it."

When he returned from the kitchen a minute later, ready for more, Lori launched into the rest of it. She slumped against the back of the couch as they talked, trying to remember everything she'd been told. Conner listened patiently as she explained what little she knew about packs, and the Glenwood pack specifically. As she did, she wondered if she ought to be revealing these people's secrets to someone else, but Conner was a wolf, too. Lori went on to explain the vision she'd had and the moon goddess they'd descended from. He only raised his eyebrows slightly when she talked about finding her soulmate.

The most difficult of all was the part about being Rex's Luna. "I came home after that. I told him I needed some time to just think about all of this. I feel awful about it, but it's a huge decision. It would change everything. And I was so worried about you, once I knew this might be something that would affect you, too." Lori wrapped her arms around him and held him tightly.

They sat like that for a while when Conner spoke up. "Mom."

"Hm?"

"I think you should go for it."

Lori let go and leaned back. "What?"

"Everything you said about being part of a pack and having people there for you. All of that." He rolled his hand through the air to encompass all that Rex had explained to her. "I've been dealing with this completely alone, and it sucks. You shouldn't have to do that, too."

"But what about all this about taking care of the pack?" she pressed. "I'd never even heard of a pack in these terms until now. I don't know that I want the responsibility."

"Who knows? Maybe you'll actually like it. You won't know until you try."

"There you go using my own advice against me again," she joked, even though she knew he was right.

"Only because it was good advice in the first place," Conner replied. "Really, Mom. You should do it."

She pursed her lips, thinking there was even more to consider than she'd originally imagined. It was like an origami piece that just kept unfolding the more you tugged at it, constantly revealing more layers. "The idea of me being with someone doesn't bother you? I mean, so soon after your dad and I split up?"

"Nah. I mean, it's a little weird to think of my mom as anything but just a mom. But I'm not worried about it otherwise. If you're meant for each other, then that's just the way it is. Actually, that's kind of a nice thought." Conner looked out the window, his eyes distant.

"What's that, honey?"

"I'm not ready yet, but someday I wouldn't mind having a family. Knowing what I am made me think that might never be possible. How could I be with someone if there's this wild monster inside of me? But you said shifters believe there's someone out there, someone specific for each one of them. That means someday I'll find that someone, too."

"I know you will." Lori held him once again, and the two of them sat in silence as the afternoon light changed in her living room. He'd been through so much, and he'd managed it all by himself. That pained her to the very center of her soul, even though she could see just how mature it'd made him.

He was right. She didn't have to do this alone.

18

COLD RAIN DRIZZLED DOWN FROM THE LOW-HANGING clouds. As Rex charged down a narrow deer path, scents from the animals that'd passed through stirred up from the damp earth. He focused on the snap and release of his muscles as he ran and the way his paws dug into the ground before pushing off again. His ears twitched, catching the sharp crack of a dead branch that had finally given up and let go.

Try as he might to keep his senses busy, none of it was enough. Rex's mind refused to clear, a state he'd been in for days now. Questions and possibilities floated through his brain, answered or forgotten as quickly as they came. His soul simply wouldn't be satisfied until he had Lori back.

His father was right. Rex had known that even

before they'd talked. He'd thought getting confirmation from the retired Alpha would be the key to acceptance, but it wasn't. Rex only found it harder to be patient and wait for Lori because now he felt all the more hopeful that she might come back to him.

But despair would dip in again. It did so now as he cut off to the right. He shoved it away, not wanting to feel sorry for himself, but impatience and grim determination took over. How long would Lori make him wait? Another day? A week? Years? She was freshly divorced and even more freshly a wolf. The logical part of him understood that she needed time, but he'd already waited so long to find her. There was nothing left for him to decide, and the fates were cruel to keep him dangling by a thread for even another day.

Turning, Rex charged up a steep slope. His haunches bunched underneath him as he launched himself upward. The rain had softened the earth, but the tree roots held it firmly enough in place to keep him from sliding backward. His muscles burned, and he pushed harder as he crested the hill and came onto the back of the property. He didn't want to wait another day, so he wouldn't. He'd go into town and find her, which wouldn't be too hard. He'd pull her into his arms and kiss her with all the passion that'd been boiling over inside him. Then he'd make her understand just how much she meant to him. He didn't know how, but he had to make her understand.

I do understand.

That glorious voice echoed in his head and made Rex slide to a halt. Mud pushed up under his claws, and he shook his paw with irritation. Rex was just at the edge of the woods and knew he'd been alone. He stepped forward, edging out of the trees and into the clearing around the packhouse.

Lori stood there in all of her snow-white glory. Her tail flicked to one side and then the other when she saw him, a gesture close enough to a wag that it made Rex's heart thunder. She was just as beautiful as he remembered. Lori had only been apart from him for a few days, yet it felt like he was seeing a vision out of a dream.

Lori, what are you doing here?

Do you want me to leave? Was that a gleam of mischief in her violet eyes?

He trotted forward. *I wasn't sure if you'd come back. I had to, Rex.*

There was something sensual about having her inside his head, but Rex wanted more. He let go of his wolf, easily slipping out of his animal form and again standing on two legs. Her own shift was smoother than it'd been the first few times, although the grimace of pain that remained on her face for a moment when she stood in front of him on two feet told him she still had a long way to go.

"I've done a lot of thinking," she said, taking a small step toward him.

He felt her hesitation. Even without being in her mind, Rex could tell she was worried. Did she think he wouldn't accept her? That he'd be angry with her for taking her time? Impatient, worried, and all sorts of other stubborn feelings, yes. But never angry, not with her. He wanted to pull her close and cover her mouth with his own to let her know the truth, but first, he needed to hear what she had to say. "And?"

Another inch forward. "There had to be a reason I came to Eugene, not just because of Conner. I could've made all sorts of decisions, but I chose the path that led me here, to you. There had to be a reason I followed that silly raven and stumbled on your pack. There had to be a reason that when I went looking for work and was just about to give up, I decided to walk into Selene's." The rain had been easily repelled by her fur, but now it soaked into her hair and made the shoulders of her sweater turn dark.

"Of all the clubs in the world, you had to come into mine," he said with a smile, still uncertain that she'd come there to give him the news he'd been waiting for.

She smiled back, and the gap between them closed a little more. "Exactly. There also must be a reason that I can't stop thinking about you. Not just because I find you attractive or because I know you understand more about my future than I do, but because I have a link with you that I've never experienced before in my life. I don't see how I ever could again."

He was close enough now that he put his hands on her arms. "You do feel it?" he asked softly as rainwater trickled down the back of his neck. She'd said it before, but he wanted to be sure.

"I really do." Her hands pressed against his chest, and she looked at him with desperation filling her dark eyes. "I admit I questioned it. There was just so much, and it was all so new. But I can see now that I have something exceptional here with you. I can accept who I am, but I can't be who I truly am without you."

He claimed her mouth with his own, her lips a warm contrast to the cold rain soaking them both through. Rex didn't care about the rain or anything else as long as he had her. His tongue slipped along the tip of hers and down its side, racing back against her teeth. He plundered her again as his hands roved around to grip her hips and pull her closer. He'd missed her so much.

Lori pulled back and rested her cheek against his, her breath silken against his ear. "Rex, I want you to mark me."

The heat of desire punched through him, hitting him hard like a fist to his stomach. He tipped his head back so that he could see her face. "You know what this means."

"Yes." Her fingers curled, clinging to him now. "It scared me at first, but I want to embrace every part of what I'm supposed to be. I've been a mother, a wife, and a partner. I think I'm qualified to be your Luna."

He kissed her again, feeling his wolf surge impatiently inside him. "You definitely are."

Keeping her gaze steadily on his, Lori tipped her head to the side.

Rex gently brushed her hair out of the way. Pulling aside the neck of her sweater, he grazed his thumb against her skin. His fangs gave him a slight sting as they descended, and he took a deep breath. This was the moment he'd been waiting for his whole life, and it was finally here. He touched his lips to her skin and bit down.

Her body tensed in his arms. She shuddered, but then relaxed against him as a low moan emanated from her throat.

Rex watched as blood pooled from the wound he'd created, its brilliance standing out as the only color in this gray world. The rain mixed with it and ran down her skin, pinkening the collar of her sweater. "Let's get you inside."

The packhouse was quiet. He kept his arm around her as they moved down the hall and straight into his den. He closed the door and guided her to the hearth, where the fire was already lit, filling the room with its glow. "Are you okay?"

His hands were slipping out from around her waist, and Lori reached up to tighten her grip on his elbows. Her eyes burned with need as she pulled him back. "Not yet." She trailed her lips across his and then down the line of his jaw, her hands clenched against his waist, keeping him close.

Not that he was interested in going anywhere. He nibbled her ear lobe, where a small amethyst stud winked at him. Just below, he could smell the blood he'd drawn. The wound was fresh, but it was quickly healing. He felt another jolt of electricity through him knowing it was there, and he pressed his lips to the mark. She rewarded him with another one of those sweet, deep sighs from her throat, and he twisted his hands in the hem of her sweater, sending the sodden knit to the floor.

She inhaled as she gently scraped her teeth against the front of his throat. Her hands worked up the front of his chest until she found the top button of his shirt, and Rex slowly felt the heat of the fire as she unfastened one after the other. That heat only intensified as she ran her hands appreciatively over his chest and up his shoulders to push away the fabric.

Their shoes clunked against the brick of the fireplace. His belt buckle jingled softly, and damp denim was added to the growing pile until Rex could see her in her full glory. He'd already experienced her once before when his craving for her could no longer hold out against her flirtatious smile and thudding heartbeat. He'd taken her, their bodies coming together to satisfy the physical need that they'd held for each other. It'd been rough and carnal, a satisfaction that had pleased them both, but now he had the time to admire her in a way he hadn't been able to while he'd had her pinned to a table.

Rex caressed her breasts, feeling the weight of them in his hands as he stroked his thumbs across her nipples. They hardened under his touch, sending lightning up his arms at knowing she responded to him. Her soft waist tucked in a bit at her ribs before expanding into the curve of her hips. He glided his hands over her luscious backside and squeezed it in his palms, reveling in it. She rested against his hardness as he held her in his arms, making his body eager for more.

They explored each other in the flickering light of the fire. Her hand against the inside of his thigh, slowly trailing upward. Her head resting on his shoulder as he found the sensitive pearl between her legs. The gentle whimpers that escaped her lips climbing in intensity and blowing across his skin as he built her higher. Her grip on him needful and curious, yet knowing.

He was so focused on the feeling of her body against him, he hardly knew how they'd managed to get to the couch. She straddled him, her core teasing him once again as she ran her hands through his hair and brought the entirety of his body to life. She lifted herself, and Rex gripped her hips as she slowly lowered again, sliding along his length.

Lori rocked her hips against him, taking him to

the hilt, and he could hardly stand the pleasure of it. His head reeled and his wolf churned. He pressed his lips to the cleft between her breasts as she moved against him, bucking and grinding. Her hair fell down around him in cool waves, and Rex closed his eyes, wanting to savor every moment of this. He smelled the smoke of the fire and tasted the salt of her skin. Lori's fingers laced behind his neck and pulled at his shoulders as he drew her nipple into his mouth, the gentle pressure creating a counterpoint rhythm to the beat of her hips against his.

When he felt her tighten and heard a sharp inhalation hiss through her teeth, Rex opened his eyes. He saw her with the firelight against her naked skin, the mark a dark shadow as her head tipped back, sending her hair cascading down her shoulders. She pulled him in and held him there as her lips parted. She was a gorgeous sight as her teeth clenched and Rex felt her contract around him. Her waves enveloped him as they pulsed through her, crashing like the ocean one after another. Her toes pressed into his knees as Lori completely lost control of her body and gave it all over to him.

Rex felt that loss of control growing within him, as well, and he gladly gave it up. Lori writhed on top of him, and a glorious tension rose within him, consuming him. As Lori's body called to him, his pressure built. He pulled her hips closer, and it finally broke free.

He held her, feeling her panting against him as she caught her breath. His wolf reached out experimentally, easily finding hers. Their bond was sealed.

EPILOGUE

"Leave your cell phone here," Lori advised. "They said there should be no artificial light at all, and I'm sure that includes screens." To be safe, she took her own cell out of her pocket, turned it on silent, and set it on the dresser.

"Should I be nervous?" Conner asked. He sat on the edge of an armchair, his fingers knotted in front of him. "I feel like I should be, but I'm not. I'm just ready to do this and see what it's like."

Lori laughed. "I can be plenty nervous for both of us."

"Are you having second thoughts?"

She sat at the vanity in the room Rex had given her to get ready and touched up her face. There was probably no need for makeup at all. Rex had seen her in almost every state imaginable, whether sweaty and injured or soaked with rain. He wouldn't care, but she wanted to look as put together as possible. It seemed like the respectful thing to do.

"No second thoughts," she replied confidently as she swiped an extra coat of mascara on. "It's just that I don't know what I'm doing. Joan and Rex went over it all with me, but I don't want to mess anything up."

"Good. I'm glad you're doing this, Mom. I like the idea of you being happy."

She glanced at him in the mirror, and when she saw how earnest he looked, she turned to face him. "You don't think I've been happy?"

"Not the way you needed to be. I mean, you had a place and a job, but I don't think that necessarily adds up to being truly happy. Ever since you decided you wanted to be with Rex, you've been different," he tried to explain. "Like before, you were always sort of on edge. You worried a lot, and you seemed like you were frustrated. It's not like that now."

She smiled, reflecting on what he'd just said. Of course those few days she'd been trying to decide whether or not to accept her destined role had been fretful. But even before that, she'd never quite settled into herself there in Eugene. It made her wonder if she'd ever really been herself, even twenty years ago. Now, life seemed fresh and new. The fact that her wolf had zapped her hot flashes and mood swings didn't hurt either. "Yeah, I guess you're right. What about you?"

"You don't have to worry about me, Mom. I've got things figured out well enough." He flapped his hand in the air to dismiss her concerns.

"As I've told you before, I'm always going to worry about you. But really, do you think you'd want to join a pack someday?" Lori was already feeling a little apprehensive about tonight, but this question made knots in her shoulders.

Conner considered it. "You know, I think I would. I mean, if there was one that would have me. The time I've been able to spend with some of the shifters here has been pretty great. Rex has offered some good advice, and Jimmy has some awesome cars."

Lori laughed, easily remembering the astonished look on Conner's face when Jimmy had brought him out to the garage and let him get behind the wheel of a sixty-nine Corvette. The Glenwoods had been more fatherly to Conner in this short span of time than Chuck had, and it both touched her and made her sad. "It's not all about cool cars, you know."

"Yeah, I know." His smile changed as he looked down at the floor. "Honestly, it's like the whole world is different now that I know I'm not the only one."

"I'm so glad, honey." Lori glanced up at the clock. "It's getting close to time. I'm going to get dressed."

"I'll wait in the living room."

Lori removed the snowy white dress that Joan had loaned her from a hanger. She'd gone to Rex's mother for advice on what to wear, and she'd seemed incredibly pleased to be asked. When she'd produced this gown, with long draping sleeves and a silver belt at the waist, Lori hadn't been too sure it was right for her. But how could she possibly say no, when Joan and the rest of the pack had already done so much for her?

She slipped it on, pleased to find a zipper in the side for easy access so she wouldn't have to embarrass Conner by asking for help. Lori turned to look in the full-length mirror mounted on the closet door and blinked in surprise. It fit her curves perfectly, hugging them just right. With the way the neckline dipped to just the right length to suit her assets, she felt feminine and sexy.

A few minutes later, she and Conner stepped out

the back door. The moon was full, casting its silvery glow on the packhouse grounds. They emerged from under a black canopy that extended from the back of the house to the edge of the woods.

"What's this all about?" Conner asked.

"I can't say that I understand everything behind it," Lori admitted, "but I'm supposed to stay out of the moonlight until we get there. It has something to do with not taking any of Selene's power without permission, which I'm guessing is also why you have to wear black. Everyone else will be, too."

"A real black-tie affair, then," Conner cracked as he held out his elbow.

She set her hand in the crook of it as they moved toward the woods. Rex had shown her the way, but that had been during the day while they had gone out in wolf form. The tightly knit branches overhead served the same function as that canopy had, thoroughly blocking out all the natural light. For a moment, she worried they would lose their way and ruin the night, but her wolf reminded her that it was still there. Lori took a deep breath and tapped into all the new capabilities she had within her now. Her wolf knew the way, and she let it guide her feet.

It was hard to tell what time it was in this darkness, and she wasn't sure how much of it had gone by when she finally spotted the clearing ahead of them. Dark figures moved within it, and her nerves zinged with energy. This was it. There was no going back now, no changing her mind. If someone had asked her a few months ago how she would've felt about a commitment like this, she would've turned and run. Lori wanted to run now, but only straight forward.

As they'd been instructed, Lori and Conner stopped just short of the clearing, where the darkness still covered them. The pack members formed a ring in the clearing, leaving just enough space by the path for one person to enter. Like Conner, they were all garbed entirely in black. Two figures stood at the very center. A pile of wood lay at her feet, ready for a fire, but it hadn't been lit. A large, flat stone sat nearby, and Lori could see that several objects occupied it, but she couldn't quite tell what any of them were. The scent of incense and herbs was heavy in the air, mixing with pine and loam.

"Selene!" cried out the figure in the center, and then it was obvious to Lori that it was Joan. She flung her hands toward the full moon overhead, her hair tumbling down the back of her black dress. "We call to you on this sacred night, asking for your guidance and blessing as we accept one of your own into our fold."

Joan chanted as she moved around the inner perimeter of the circle, but Lori couldn't understand the words. Another figure followed her, repeating the same syllables. Judging by the voice, it was Dawn. Their hands moved through the air as they went. Joan sliced into it with a feather, and Dawn followed behind with a fat bundle of smoking sage. Now Lori understood where the incense smell had come from and remembered Joan saying something about cleansing the space for their ritual.

When they finished, the two women returned to the center of the circle. Dawn clasped her hands in front of her, waiting patiently, while Joan once again lifted her voice. "Who among us brings a new soul into our collective, a new strength to join us and share in our abundance?"

"I do." Rex's deep voice thundered through the clearing, sending a shiver down Lori's spine. Even in the dark, he was just as handsome. His hard jawline was impossible to miss at any distance, and even the darkness couldn't hide those broad shoulders. He stepped forward from the circle's edge, joining his mother and sister. "I ask Selene and the Glenwood pack to accept Lori Jensen as my Luna."

This was her cue. Lori let go of Conner's elbow and stepped forward. She heard him do as he'd been asked, also coming forward just enough to fill the gap in front of the path and close the circle. Faint gasps came from all around her.

Alarmed and feeling their eyes on her, Lori stepped forward until she reached Joan. "What's wrong?" she whispered.

The older woman pulled her close. "Look down, dear. You're just divine."

Lori did, and the next gasp came from her own throat. She expected the pale dress to stand out in the darkness, but not like this. The moonlight picked out the fine threads, illuminating them in an iridescent display of purples, blues, greens, and silver. It was, she realized, the same look that Selene's cape had in her vision as she'd guided her chariot. The beauty was remarkable, and she gaped at Joan as she tried to decide what to say.

Joan winked. "I thought you might like that little effect. Now go on."

Hoping her concerns hadn't derailed the ceremony too much, Lori moved to stand at Rex's side. His hand slipped easily into hers. This divorced single mom from Chinook may have never stood with a pack of wolves and a couple of witches under the full moon before, but everything felt far more natural than she ever could've imagined. Rex was warm at her side, a solid force of comfort that she was quickly learning how to lean against. She smiled up at him in the moonlight.

He dipped his head down next to her ear. "You're absolutely radiant."

"You're not so bad yourself."

Joan moved so that she stood in front of the pair. "Lori, you're a descendent of Selene herself. You're one of us, even if you haven't been a part of our pack until now. No one can doubt that you qualify to become our Luna. Do you understand the responsibility?"

She lifted her head, making sure that everyone could hear her. "Yes."

"And do you *accept* this responsibility?" Joan asked.

Lori understood the difference. She'd discussed it for hours with Rex, Joan, Jimmy, and even Conner. In the end, she was the only one who could decide. "I do."

It was Rex's turn to address the assemblage. "Glenwood pack, I have served faithfully as your Alpha. You have put your trust in me, and now I am humbled to put my trust in you. Do you accept Lori, my mate, as your Luna?"

The next moment of silence made Lori's bones tremble. She'd never really thought about what would happen if they said no.

Brody stood next to Conner, where he'd filled the gap. Deliberately, he took one step forward. The person next to him did the same, and so did the third. One by one, every pack member moved forward to show their approval. It ended with Max, who stood on the opposite side of Conner and gave Lori a nod as he took his step. Conner remained where he was on the edge of the clearing.

Lori's thready heartbeat slowed slightly, but this next part was the one that had worried her the most.

Joan smiled. "Our new Luna will guide us and care for us as she accepts our own guidance and care. We would ask for Selene's final blessing now, but it is my understanding that our Luna has a request from us tonight."

Forcing her breath to cooperate, Lori looked at the members of her new pack. "I do not come alone. I ask that you accept my pack into yours." She looked straight across the circle at Conner.

His eyes went wide in the moonlight, his shoulders

jerking slightly with shock. Conner glanced nervously at the other members of the Glenwood pack. He licked his lips as he looked at the ground, composing himself. When he looked up again, the moonlight shimmered in the tears that had formed in his eyes.

Max took a step backward. The man next to him did the same, and the entire process of Lori's approval was repeated in reverse. Brody was the last, and he moved into place next to Conner. Trying to be subtle, Brody offered his knuckles in a fist bump.

"And so he is a part of us," Joan announced. "We take our final blessing from Selene to unite us under her power and guidance."

Rex, Lori, and Dawn rejoined the circle. With a silver goblet in her hand, Joan approached. Lori could tell the goblet's contents were heavily scented with herbs and oils as the witch dipped her finger into it and touched the center of Lori's forehead at her third eye. She did the same to Rex and then continued on.

Lori tried to watch, pleased that it had all gone so well and eager to see the conclusion, but her vision clouded. That same dizzying, detached feeling that had come upon her before took her once again, and she was no longer in the clearing with the Glenwood pack. The woods were there, but different.

Selene herself stood in front of her. Gone were the chariot and horses, no longer needed for battle, but her cape was just as brilliant as it had been before. The goddess stepped toward Lori, smiling. "You are one of us now, but you have always been. Take care of them for me." Her hand reached forward, and her fingertip touched the same spot on her forehead.

Lori was sent back before she could ask any questions. She leaned into Rex, who held her upright. At least she hadn't fallen to the ground this time.

"How are you doing?" he asked quietly. "None of us were sure how that would go for you, being who you are."

She pushed herself upright. "I'm okay. I think."

"It's a different experience for everyone," he explained quietly. "Will you tell me later?"

Later. There would be so many laters between them now that they were together. It was an idea that made her feel warm and happy inside. "Of course."

Joan had once again returned to the center of the circle. "Selene's blessings are upon us. Let the feast begin!"

The fire in the center was lit, and tables of food

were brought into the clearing as the music started. It was a full-on party now.

Conner came to find her. "Mom, what was that all about? You scared the hell out of me!"

"I'm sorry, honey. I wanted it to be a surprise."

"It was," he confirmed. "And then I didn't know if they accepted me because they were stepping backward. Then, thanks to Brody, I realized it meant they were joining me."

"Did I do the wrong thing?" she asked. "You always could've said no."

"No way, Mom. Thank you." He kissed her cheek and started eyeing one of the food tables. "I'm hungry."

He moved off to eat and converse with his new fellow packmates. Lori, her hand in Rex's, followed after him. "I knew this year was going to be different. I just didn't know how different."

"Good different?" her mate asked as he filled a plate for her.

"Definitely."

Rex had insisted she was special because of her heritage. Lori knew she was special, but not because of that.

It was because she'd finally found her destiny, and because of the people who loved her.

She was finally home.

THE END

If you enjoyed Rex and Lori's story, read on for a preview of Brody and Robin's story, *Wolf's Midlife Bite*!

BRODY

"Brody, I could really use your help!"

Immediately, Brody dropped his pencil and shot to his feet. Adrenaline coursed through his veins, and his wolf was ready. "What's up?"

Poppy smiled at him from the doorway of his booth. "I pulled you out of a sketch again, didn't I?"

"Shit." The last time Poppy had asked for help, the frat boy she'd been tattooing thought being alone in her booth meant he could get more than just artwork. She had plenty of bite and knew how to put just about any customer in their place, but her small stature tended to make men think they could take things further. That didn't seem to be the case right now. "You're good?"

"With that," she said, knowing what he meant.

"I'm just running behind. My next appointment just got here, but the shading on this sleeve is taking way longer than I thought it would."

"Squirmer?" Brody had caught a glimpse of the muscled man when he'd come in a couple of hours ago, his head thrown back and his shoulders wide.

"Yup," she confirmed quietly. "He's asked me to take so many breaks, I'll be lucky if I finish by the end of the week."

That figured. It happened all the time in their shop, and Poppy tended to overbook herself. "What's your next one getting?"

"Just a small coverup." Poppy handed him her original drawing and the stencil, which she already had ready to go. "Can I send her in?"

It wasn't anything particularly exciting, just a bird flying out of a cage, but he was more than capable. Brody took a wistful glance at the pencil drawing he'd been lost in before Poppy had asked for his help. He'd made a smudge when he'd dropped his pencil, but he could fix that later. The tattoos were what paid the bills, anyway. "Sure."

He prepped his booth while Poppy explained the situation to her customer. Brody was filling a cap with black ink when he heard the shuffle of footsteps and looked up.

She made his breath catch in his throat. Her strawberry blonde hair fell in delicate waves to her jawline, and her bright green eyes easily picked up the intense light of the booth. She hung back a little, hugging an arm around her waist.

"Come on in," he said, hoping he sounded casual even though he definitely didn't feel that way inside. Brody saw all sorts of people in this line of work, and at this point, they were all just canvases for his artwork. But this one was making his wolf churn inside him. He realized he'd overfilled the ink cap and cursed quietly to himself.

"Um, I don't know," she hedged, taking only one step further toward the chair. "Maybe I should reschedule with Poppy for another time."

"You'd probably have to wait a while before you could get back in with her," Brody replied. "She's usually booked out for a couple of months."

His potential customer bit her lip and nodded. "Yeah, I guess I already knew that. Why aren't *you*?"

Brody found himself smiling at the sassy question. It caught him off-guard, but he liked it. "I am, actually, but I purposely schedule some free time to catch up on my artwork."

"Oh." Her eyes lifted to the paintings and sketches lining the walls of the booth. "I see."

He was used to people checking out his work. It was his job, after all, and the more confidence people had in his skill, the more likely they were to come to him. It also meant they paid more. Now, though, he felt oddly exposed. He tipped his head toward the chair. "You can stay or reschedule with Poppy. It's up to you."

"Um. I guess so." She moved slowly as though she were trying to force her feet forward. "I'm sorry for being so weird. It's just that I was planning on having a female artist. No offense to you, it's just..." She gestured toward her body.

Brody's eyes landed on the spot she referred to, just inside her hipbone. People got tattoos all over their bodies, and it was his job to figure out how the planes of that canvas suited the artwork. It was all routine, yet he felt his heart jump into his throat.

"I've seen *everything* over the last few decades as a tattoo artist. Trust me, you have nothing to worry about," he assured her as he closed the booth's door for her privacy. "Why don't you have a seat. I see you've got leggings on. Good choice. You can just roll down the top and show me what we're covering up." He washed up, snapped on a pair of gloves, and grabbed a paper towel.

"Okay." Her breath became ragged as she tried to

do as he asked. She wiggled in the chair as she fought with the waistband of her leggings, trying to show him her tattoo without exposing anything else.

Brody tried not to look, knowing that would only make things worse, but it was clear she wasn't making any progress. "Can I help?" he asked.

She let out a frustrated sigh. "Don't bother. It's just not going to happen. I'm sorry."

"Come on, don't be so hard on yourself." With expert hands, he pulled down one side of her leggings to expose the "Property of JC" tattoo just inside her right hipbone. To keep the stretchy fabric in place, he tugged it down on the left side as well so it wouldn't just roll back up. Tucking the paper towel around the roll he'd created, he nodded at his own work. "There."

"Um, isn't that a little far?" Her face flushed as red as her hair as she reached down to cover herself.

He hadn't meant to embarrass her, but he had a job to do. "I have to be able to get to the tattoo to cover it, you know."

"Right."

He rubbed down the area with an alcohol prep pad. "What's your name?" It was usually a question he asked *before* he pulled a woman's pants down, but whatever. Maybe small talk would help.

"Robin. Wait, what are you doing now?"

He stopped with the disposable razor in the air over her skin. "Shaving you."

"Oh, god. I'm not that hairy down there, am I?"

Brody chuckled as he went about his work. "No. I have to do this, no matter how fine the hair is. You won't get a good clean tat, otherwise." He held her soft skin taught as he ran the razor over it.

The smell of peaches mixed with the warm, velvety scent of her skin. She was human, he could tell, but her scent was entirely different from the others. Something about her was driving his wolf crazy. Brody focused on his goal, eyeing the fuzzy, crooked letters inked into her skin as he ran an alcohol wipe over them once again. "Where did you have this done?"

An angry huff emanated from her throat. "You don't want to know."

"I probably already do," he murmured as he picked up the stencil. "I guess that means you're not going to tell me who JC is, either."

She pressed her lips together.

He rolled a shoulder as he carefully placed the stencil. "You don't have to, but people usually have some pretty big life events attached to their tattoos. Coverups are like therapy."

Robin was silent for a moment, and Brody could tell just by having the side of his hand against her that every muscle in her body was tense. "JC is my ex," she finally admitted.

"Mm." Not a surprise. He wouldn't have ever done a tattoo like that for someone. The only names he was comfortable with permanently inking onto clients were those of kids, pets, or loved ones who'd passed on. It was pretty safe that those relationships wouldn't change, unlike this one.

"He was the one who did it, too," she volunteered.

"I kind of figured that." The faded, blown-out lines were the first clue, along with the inconsistently-sized letters. Brody grabbed a hand mirror and showed her the stencil. "How's that?"

It was obvious that she'd been trying to avoid looking at him or what he was doing, but she gave a blink of surprise as she looked at the reflection. "Is that really going to cover the whole thing?

"Like it was never there," he replied confidently. Coverups could be a bitch, but Poppy had done a good job of designing this one so that the cage's base covered JC's masterpiece completely.

"Then yeah." A hint of a smile played on her lips.

"Cool. I'm going to lay you down to make this a

little easier." He pushed the foot pedal that reclined the chair all the way back. It jolted to life, making her curves jiggle a little. Brody really needed to keep his focus on the work. "So, was this your idea?"

Robin snorted a little as she adjusted herself on the chair. She had her arms pulled up over her chest to keep them out of the way, but at least they were relaxed now. "No, not exactly. JC was super controlling, and he liked the idea. He kept bugging the hell out of me to do it, especially once he'd ordered a kit so that he could start practicing to be an artist. I was young and dumb, and he managed to convince me one night after I'd been drinking. The evidence of what happened is all right there."

Picking up his machine, Brody tested the mechanism before dipping the needle in black ink. He'd seen all sorts of bad tats, but this one pissed him off. It was total crap, for one thing, and no one should be tattooing at home, especially on someone under the influence. But it wasn't just the ethics, cleanliness, or even the lack of artistry. Some asshole had put his stamp on this woman. He adjusted his grip, forcing himself to loosen up a little, but his wolf wasn't having it. The beast lashed out inside him, snarling at the idea of her being anyone's property but his own.

"So, is this JC an artist somewhere now?" Brody asked, almost hoping he was so he could go find him when he was done.

"Nope," she said with a snicker. "That was just one of the many great things he thought he was going to do. He did this one, and then he did what was supposed to be a dog on his friend's back. It looked more like Cousin Itt from *The Addams Family*, and he gave up."

The buzzing of the machine echoed through the room as Brody ran a long, clean line around the outside of the cage. "Sounds like a fucking winner."

"Well, you know what they say. There's a reason he's an ex."

And it was a damn good thing he was. The lines at the corners of Brody's eyes deepened as he tried to focus on his work, but he could just imagine what he'd do to this prick if he were still around. His wolf liked the idea of tearing him apart, piece by piece. He started on the inner lines of the cage, not even needing to ask Robin what this symbolized. She was free now.

He liked to lose himself in his artistry, but it wouldn't happen today. Not while he was so close to her. Even bent over her like this, with his hands touching her, his face so close to her delicate skin, it wasn't enough. Her scent was utterly intoxicating, tempting his wolf to make an appearance. He needed a distraction. "So, where do you work?"

"Oh. I'm a dental hygienist."

"Yeah? How long have you been doing that?" Brody swapped to his other machine with a shading needle, filling in the base of the birdcage and covering JC's work. It filled him with deep satisfaction to make those words disappear.

"Oh, just about twenty years now." She was finally starting to relax, her muscles loosening the longer she lay there. "I went to hygiene school right after high school, and I've been cleaning teeth ever since."

Next came the bird itself, and he switched to a bright blue ink. "You know, I've got a tooth that's been bothering me. You came to see me at my office, so maybe I should come see you at yours."

"Well, we're usually booked about two months in advance."

Brody looked up and saw the sarcastic smile on her face. "So I hear. I guess I'll have to make an appointment right away, then."

"You should," she smiled. "How's it looking?"

"You're done." Brody wiped down her skin, knowing this wouldn't be the last time he'd touch it.

"Are you serious? I hardly even felt a thing!" She pushed herself up onto her elbows.

Scooting back on his stool, Brody hit the foot pedal to raise her back to a seated position. "That's what happens when you come to a professional. Go check it out." He pointed toward the full-length mirror in the back corner of his booth.

Robin's modesty seemed to fly out the window as she raced over to the mirror with her waistband still rolled down, holding her tummy up to study her new work. She was too focused on what Brody had done for her. "This is incredible. I can't thank you enough."

"It's not a problem. I've got some aftercare sheets for you, and you can always call if you have any questions." Brody stripped off his gloves and pulled the papers out of a nearby file, the standard for every customer. But that only gave him another minute with her before he sent her out to pay at the front.

"Thanks." Adjusting her pants, she reached for her purse. "And here's the card for my office, if you really do want to have that tooth evaluated."

His fingers brushed hers as he took it, energy crackling between them and straight up his arm. "I'll see you there."

Universe Collection (Includes Daddy Dragon Guardians and Shifters Between Worlds)

More Shifter Romance Series

Beverly Hills Dragons Series

Dragons of Sin City Series

Dragons of the Darkblood Secret Society Series

Packs of the Pacific Northwest Series

Compilations

Forever Fated Mates Collection

Shifter Daddies Collection

Early Novellas

Mated By The Dragon Boss

Claimed By The Werebears of Green Tree

Bearer of Secrets

Rogue Wolf

ABOUT THE AUTHOR

Steamy shifter romance author Meg Ripley is a Seattle native who's relocated to New England. She can often be found whipping up her next tale curled up in a local coffee house with a cappuccino and her laptop.

Download *Alpha's Midlife Baby,* the steamy prequel to Meg's Fated Over Forty series, when you sign up for the Meg Ripley Insiders newsletter!

Sign up by visiting www.authormegripley.com

Connect with Meg

amazon.com/Meg-Ripley/e/B00Z8I9AXW
tiktok.com/@authormegripley
facebook.com/authormegripley
instagram.com/megripleybooks
bookbub.com/authors/meg-ripley
goodreads.com/megripley
pinterest.com/authormegripley

Printed in Great Britain
by Amazon

43430234R00148